# *changed by you*

## MINNESOTA MAMMOTHS

### BOOK 3

## BRENDA ROTHERT

*one*

## ALICE

"Are you serious? This room is the size of my *closet* at my beach house. And my closet has more windows," my boss Farrah, says cringing dramatically as she looks around the space.

It's a beautiful room decorated in white with pops of pale yellow. The queen bed is layered with pillows and a crisp, bright-white duvet. A few framed vintage travel posters for coastal California are perfectly lined up on the walls.

"Check out that view, though." I walk over and open the doors that lead onto a small balcony with two chairs and a tiny table, letting in the sound of the crashing waves.

She sighs, unimpressed. "Yeah, it's nice. And I guess I won't be in here much, anyway. I'll be too busy with JP."

"Exactly." I side-eye the room's small closet. "Which clothes are most important for the next few days? I'll unpack what you'll need and store the rest of the luggage in my room."

Not that I have any extra space. The producers of *Celebrity Love Malibu*, the show Farrah is about to start filming here, balked when her agent told them she'd need a room for her personal assistant. The other fifteen celebrities on the show will all manage the five-week stay here without someone to bring them Starbucks and puree fresh fruit face masks, but not Farrah. And since it's a sixteen-bedroom house and there are sixteen contestants, the producers had to squeeze me into the house's staff quarters by moving a chef's assistant to a hotel. My room is roughly the size of a postage stamp and it smells like fish.

"I don't know yet." Farrah shrugs. "The producers said they want their wardrobe people to dress me, but I'm thinking no. I'll probably need Cara."

My brows fly up in alarm. "Cara? Have you talked to her about it?"

Farrah laughs. "Of course not, that's your job."

I suppress a sigh and start typing out a text to Cara, a boutique owner who has been helping choose and order clothes for Farrah for more than a year. She's in demand and her schedule is always booked, but Farrah expects her to be available anytime.

This is my own fault. I know how Farrah is about clothes. I should have asked her about it when she signed the contract to do the show.

"I'm starving," Farrah says, sitting down on the bed to look at her phone. "Can you get me some tuna sushi? And a lavender water?"

"Of course. I'll go right now." I duck out of the room as quickly as I can, eager for a break.

Some people think actors hardly work, but the ones at the top of their game, like Farrah, work very hard. She starts her days at sunrise with yoga and meditation, which she insists I do with her. Then, a small breakfast and a ninety-minute workout. Those things are nonnegotiable unless she's filming and the director can't accommodate it.

When she's not filming, her schedule is still full. She's developing a line of cosmetics, and she has meetings for that and all sorts of other things, lunches and dinners with friends, and parties.

So freaking many parties. I'm an introvert and I hate everything about them. The cackling. The frivolity. The phoniness. Farrah rarely asks me to go to those with her because she doesn't want to seem high maintenance.

Those are the evenings I recharge in bed with a book or catch up on her emails. Working for Farrah is demanding. We tried splitting it into two jobs--both of which were still a lot--but she complained so much about the other assistants that after going through several, she offered to triple my salary to work for her basically around the clock.

It's not as bad as it sounds. When she's filming, she's sometimes occupied for sixteen hours a day or more, and I can pretty much do what I want as long as she can reach me by text. And it's worth it to make the money I do at age twenty-six.

"Hey...Farrah's assistant, right?" A middle-aged man with a baseball hat and a beard stops me as I'm about to walk out the beach house's front door.

"Alice. Yes."

"Can you ask her to meet us in the library for a production meeting at two?"

The *what*? Did he just say there's a *library* here? Is this heaven masquerading as a beach house?

"Sure can." I smile and wave at him, texting Farrah on my walk to the car.

Occasionally Farrah likes to ride places with me, even though she has a driver. She needs to wear a hat and glasses to disguise herself when we go, but she still likes to get out. That's why I always get a rental she'd enjoy, and this time, I went with a white convertible Bronco.

I had to park more than a quarter of a mile from the house because of the show's filming and security zones, but the walk to the car is nice on this bright June day.

Sunny California is a welcome change from the Drakensberg Mountains in South Africa, where Farrah was filming a movie until it wrapped six days ago. We had to watch out for leopards there, and I couldn't get the chai tea lattes I'm semidependent on.

When I reach the Bronco, I text my mom.

*Alice: Hey, how is he today? And how are you?*

I know she won't respond immediately, so I tuck my phone into my bag. I tie my dark shoulder-length hair back into a ponytail so I can enjoy the ride without hair in my face. Then I take the car's top down and look for a local sushi place on my phone.

There's one that looks good about five miles away. I start my drive, admiring the modern, sprawling mansions around me. They're all set far back from the road, landscaping and trees used to create privacy. This is exactly the kind of neighborhood people would drive through just to check out the houses--if they could.

But it's gated. I had to submit my driver's license and get a background check just to be able to come in. Farrah's face gets her into places like this. She just smiles and waves and is immediately recognized as one of the most famous actresses in the world.

I don't resent it. Being recognized and approached everywhere sounds terrible to me. I'm lucky--I get to experience a lot of things alongside Farrah, but I don't have to deal with being the famous person myself.

Experiences like hiking in the Drakensberg Mountains which was a once-in-a-lifetime opportunity. My parents were floored when I FaceTimed them so they could see a vervet monkey in a tree one day, so close I could make out the tiniest details of its face.

I've also been sailing on mega yachts, had dinner at the Eiffel Tower, and skydived. Being Farrah's assistant is exhausting at times, but it's never boring.

Parking is impossible near the sushi place, so I end up walking a couple of blocks. When I step inside, there are people waiting for their orders, but no one is in line to place an order.

I smile at the guy behind the counter.

"What can I get you?" he asks.

"Is your tuna sashimi grade?"

"Yes. Yellowfin."

"Great. I'll take a tuna roll, please. No sauce, wasabi or ginger, not even on the side. And I only want two pieces of the roll in the container. And no Styrofoam. You can put it in a paper cup if you need to."

He lowers his brows, clearly questioning my sanity. I'm used to it.

"Only two pieces?" He gestures to a case of already-prepared individual pieces of sushi.

I shake my head. "No, I need it freshly made, please. I'll pay for the entire roll, but I only want two pieces."

He shrugs. A guy in line shoots me a judgmental glance, probably over Farrah's neurotic sushi order.

Having an entire roll in the container is too tempting, she says. She finds two pieces "satisfying". But if I get an entire roll so she can save some for later, it doesn't feel like a real meal to her.

That's because two pieces of sushi *aren't* a meal, but I don't argue with her. She's expected to look perfect and that creates a lot of pressure.

Once I have the sushi, it takes me almost thirty minutes to get to Whole Foods, with traffic getting heavier as it gets later. I know Whole Foods sells Voss water, though, and that's the only kind Farrah drinks. I pick up two dozen large glass bottles of it and the store's entire stock of organic lemons and dried lavender.

When I get back to the beach house, I'll prepare enough waters to last Farrah today and tomorrow. That'll take all the lemons I bought because I slice up three for every water and add in a couple sprigs of lavender.

Hopefully I can hit up a farmers' market tomorrow when she's working and get more lemons.

I check my phone before leaving the Whole Foods parking lot and see that Farrah has texted me three times.

*Farrah: Sushi???*

*Farrah: Wilting away here...*

*Farrah: the show's MUA asked if she can pluck my brows!! Can you even?? I don't even know you, rando MUA, but sure, go ahead and potentially ruin my entire face...*

I shake my head, smiling at her overly dramatic reaction, and text back.

*Alice: Whole Foods was a long drive. Heading back to the house now.*

*Farrah: Okay, hurry.*

*Farrah: I saw JP!! His smile made my ovaries quiver. Sooo glad you taught me that football stuff!*

I set my phone down without responding because traffic is looking nightmarish at this point and I don't want to waste any time.

When Farrah's agent told her who the other contestants on the show were, she immediately decided to end up with JP Covington, a pro football quarterback. I made her study guides about the game and quizzed her for hours until she had it down. Then we started watching old games and I explained things to her and then made her explain things to me.

It only takes me twenty minutes to get back to my previous parking place. I replace the Bronco's top and load the water and lemons into empty tote bags I keep in my purse. Everything just barely fits, and the bags are heavy.

"Badge?" a guy monitoring the security perimeter asks me.

It's in my purse, so I set my bags down and get it out to show him.

After scrutinizing it, he says, "You need to wear that at all times, please."

"Okay." I put the lanyard over my head and pick my stuff back up.

A woman jogs past us and I recognize her as Misty Meyers, an Olympic gymnast. The security guy ignores her. But I guess that tracks because she's one of the contestants on the show.

When the beach house's entrance comes into view, I see a couple of cars in the unloading zone. I head for the side entrance where the kitchen is, hoping to avoid running into people on my way into the house. My shoulders are burning from the weight of all the glass bottles.

"Go long!" a deep male voice calls out. Then he laughs and says, "Jesus, Lorenzo. Is that what hockey players consider long?"

"Your mom says it's the biggest she's ever had!" The man who responds is huge, and he's running in reverse so he can keep his eyes on the football arcing toward us.

Like directly toward us. Everything seems to be in slow motion as I realize what's about to happen.

"Hey!" I cry in alarm. "You're g--"

It's too late. He barrels into me, knocking the bags from my arms and sending me flying.

## two

## DALTON

"Oh shit." I kneel down beside the woman I just knocked over. "I'm so sorry, I didn't even see you. Are you okay?"

She groans softly and lifts her head. I instinctively put a palm on her shoulder. "No, stay down. Don't try to move."

She turns over and gets on one knee. "I have to go. Farrah--"

"Sit."

She meets my gaze, defiance flickering in her hazel eyes. But she does sit still.

"Can you follow my finger with your eyes?"

She does, gingerly rubbing one of her knees. Guilt stabs me in the chest. I had no idea she was there, but that doesn't excuse what I did. I obviously hurt her, and it's even worse that I did it horsing around with JP.

"Okay, that's good. Now follow my finger up and down."

"I'm fine." She pushes up on a hand, trying to get up. "I have to get my boss her lunch."

"You could have a concussion."

She scoffs. "I said I'm fine."

She's pretty. Her eyes are a mix of green, brown and gold, framed by thick, dark lashes. Her hair is pulled back at the nape of her neck and she's wearing plain jean shorts and a T-shirt, but it's impossible not to notice she has a great body. She's a natural beauty.

I don't recognize her, and I've looked up every contestant on the show I'm not familiar with.

When I stand up and offer her a hand, she lets me help her into a standing position. At six foot one, I'm a solid seven inches taller than her. I keep holding onto her hand, furrowing my brow.

"I'm really sorry. I'm Dalton, by the way."

"Alice. And don't worry about it."

She releases my hand and I instantly miss the

soft, warm feel of her skin on mine. As she walks over to the bags that flew from her arms, she limps slightly. I cringe, knowing her knee hurts and it's my fault.

"Here, let me," I say as she bends to pick up a bag.

I hurry over and get it for her. It's heavy as shit and looks like it has glass bottles of water in it. There's a plastic sack on the ground that was underneath the other one, and I hand her the lighter one, keeping the heavy one in my hand.

She opens the sack and takes out a brown paper container that's smashed flat. When she flips the lid up, she groans and glares at me.

"Great," she says in a sulky tone. "There's no way she's eating that."

"I'll replace it."

Her eyes widen with frustration. "Can you replace it within five minutes? She's already hangry."

"It's only..." I glance at the container. "Two pieces of sushi. Or it was, I guess. Now it's more like pureed sushi."

My grin gets me nowhere with Alice. She ignores me and reaches for the other bag on the ground.

"And the lavender is smashed, too." She looks at me, her eyes narrowed in a death glare.

"I'll replace it all," I assure her. "But first, we need to figure out what's going on with your knee. There's a doctor on call. Let me figure out how to reach him."

"Hey, Lorenzo!" JP calls out from the other side of the lawn. "We're supposed to get inside for a meeting with the producers!"

"You go ahead!"

"You're not coming?"

"I'll get there when I can!"

I can't just leave Alice here by herself. I'm texting a production assistant about reaching the doctor the producers have on call when I notice her walking away from me, still limping.

"Hey, wait," I call out.

"Just find someone to leave the water in the kitchen for me." She turns back to look at me, shielding her eyes from the sun with her hand. "I have to go get more sushi and lavender."

"No, let me do that."

Her lips curve up in a smile. "Trust me, you won't get the sushi order right. And you're a contestant on the show. You can't just leave."

I sigh, aggravated. Even though I must look like

a douchebag to her right now, I'm actually not. I don't knock women to the ground and leave them injured and alone.

"Let me Door Dash the stuff."

She turns around and starts walking again. "That won't work."

"At least let me pay you for it!"

Alice calls over her shoulder. "It's Farrah's money. Don't worry about it."

She has to be talking about Farrah Reed. Maybe Alice is one of the show's production assistants.

"Dalton!" Ben, who definitely *is* a production assistant for the show, is waving me over to the house's main entrance.

I look back at Alice again and then jog over to Ben.

"They're waiting on you so they can start the meeting," he says.

My mind is still on my run-in with Alice.

"Does Alice work for the show?"

He wrinkles his brow, confused. "Alice? I don't know of anyone named Alice."

I gesture to the woman walking away from the house. He squints, trying to make her out.

"Oh, her. That's Farrah's assistant."

My brows shoot up. "Farrah brought her own assistant?"

"So I'm told. But listen, you have to get into the meeting. Let's go."

I shake my head. "Listen, I was playing catch with JP and I ran into Alice. I think her knee is hurt. I want a doctor to look her over."

"Yeah, we'll take care of it." He puts a hand on my back. "Seriously, you have to get to this meeting. We plan to start shooting tonight and we can't afford to fall behind."

I glance over my shoulder at Alice, who's passing a security guard, still limping. I'll have to check in on her later. Ben leads the way to the meeting, and I follow.

"For the rivalry between you and JP, we want it to be lighthearted. Little barbs between the two of you. I have some examples if you need them."

I keep my game face on as Alex, one of the producers of *Celebrity Love Malibu*, tells me about the plans producers have for this season of the show.

"So this show is...scripted? My agent didn't tell me that."

Alex waves a hand, dismissing my concern. "Nah, it's not scripted. We just have some directions we like to lead you guys to make for better television. It would be boring if everyone liked each other, right?" He laughs. "We like to keep the tension as taut as a swimsuit model's stomach. We have what we call a Three-Legged Stool of Tension." He lists them off on his fingers. "Chemistry. Love Triangles. Rivalries. You and JP will fall into the rivalry category, but it'll be a passive-aggressive rivalry. We have to keep your team owners and fans happy, and we respect that."

I blow out a breath. I should have known this show wouldn't be all fun and games. When my agent told me about it, he said the producers of the show had approached the executives in charge of pro hockey and asked them to recommend a player who met the criteria they were looking for.

I assumed the criteria were one, single and two, willing. But now I'm not so sure. The woman in charge of public relations for the league came to Minneapolis, my team's home city, last week to meet with me and the PR people for the Mammoths, my team.

Rita was clear about her expectations for my appearance on the show. I'm supposed to be likable and charming. Make viewers see hockey players as good guys they can root for. The league expects to see correlations between my episodes of the show and way more people following and checking out pro hockey's social media pages.

"I'll talk to JP and see what I can do," I tell Alex.

"Great. But don't rehearse anything. We want this to all seem organic."

Organic. Right. The producers had a meeting with all sixteen contestants where they hit a few high points about the filming schedule for this week, and then they started taking us one and two people at a time for other meetings. This is my first one, and I'm already not looking forward to the others.

Alex looks down at the iPad that has his notes on it. "As far as partners, we'd really like to see some initial chemistry between you and June Calloway."

I suppress a groan. "The TikTok influencer?"

Ugh. I looked her up when I got the cast list. She talks nonstop and looks like a high school kid.

"Right. June is twenty, so she can't legally drink. It would be great if you'd bring her a virgin cocktail tonight at the party."

I just stare at Alex for a few seconds. "Dude, I'm

twenty-nine. I don't date women who aren't old enough to drink."

He smiles. "No, it won't go that far. No sex or anything. We just want to see a spark, you know? It works a lot better when viewers see connections happen, but then, in subsequent shows, there's chemistry with others. We want them talking on socials about who should be together and why. It's best if they're guessing until the end."

I shift in my chair, one of about a dozen arranged around a stone firepit outside the beach house. "So this isn't about who I actually have chemistry with?"

He shrugs. "It could be. We have contestants who met on this show and ended up dating afterward. We even had a couple get married. But no, we can't just leave things to unfold on their own, or it wouldn't be good television."

I nod, cringing inside at the thought of flirting with a twenty-year-old who's obsessed with herself. June's videos are all about her skin, her face, her body, her nails...even her fucking pores. Apparently she's not a fan of them. But Rita made it clear that I have to do my assigned job on this show, so I will.

"Questions?" Alex asks.

"No, I don't think so."

"Okay, so go shower and get changed. Mallory is your wardrobe person. You can get your clothes for tonight from her. Then, report to makeup. We'll start shooting the cocktail party at six fifteen sharp."

"Makeup? And I can't wear my own clothes?"

A flicker of annoyance passes over Alex's face. "The makeup won't show. It's just so you aren't shiny or blotchy on camera--every contestant has to do it. And not all clothes look good on camera. Just trust the professionals to handle this stuff, okay? The actors are all used to it. I forget that the athletes aren't."

I scrub a hand down my face. "Yeah, okay."

"Great. Remember, lots of smiling tonight. Lots of energy. Give me *wistful and hoping to fall in love* vibes."

I force a smile. I was really just hoping to have a good time here, have some beach house sex and maybe come out of it with a famous girlfriend I like a lot. But they won't be filming us the entire time, so hopefully, I can still get what I really want when the cameras are off.

*three*

## ALICE

Dalton Lorenzo looks *ridiculous*.

It's a shame, really. He's got a body that doesn't stop. He's tall, broad-shouldered and lean, even the visible parts of his legs defined with muscle. But put a wild-patterned Hawaiian shirt with too many buttons undone on the man, and he looks like a porn star. All he needs is a bushy stache.

His shorts are fine--just plain khaki. And his simple Birkenstock sandals are also fine. That shirt, though. There are so many buttons undone that I can see the first few inches of his dark chest hair. He really should be standing beneath a disco ball.

JP doesn't look much better. He's wearing a pastel pink and blue striped polo that belongs at a gender reveal party. But like Dalton, his body helps make up for his unfortunate apparel. One of the other contestants is a rock star, and he's so thin he looks like a teenage boy next to Dalton and JP.

Of course, Farrah looks fabulous. She's wearing a sleeveless pale-yellow dress that shows off her golden skin. The producers insisted she wear something from the show's wardrobe, but she fought to wear something she actually likes instead of what the wardrobe person picked out for her.

Hmm. Maybe Dalton and JP were dressed by the wardrobe people. I have nothing against JP, but Dalton deserves to look embarrassing on national television. My knee still hurts because of that asshole. Ice didn't help at all. Farrah was practically feral with hunger by the time I got back from my second shopping trip, so I had to talk her down before I could take care of my knee.

"Action!"

I freeze in my chair near the show's production people, reflexively knowing that when the cameras are rolling, I can't sniffle, sneeze or even breathe hard. I have to be completely silent, or I won't be allowed to stay during filming. And I know from past experience that my life will be much easier if I can watch the filming. Farrah will want to break down every interaction and conversation she has tonight, and it's so much better if I actually see them instead of her relaying her versions to me.

We once had a forty-five-minute conversation about whether a costar gave her a dirty look. When people look at Farrah, they see a confident, stunning woman without a care in the world. But truthfully, she has the same insecurities and neuroses as the rest of us.

The contestants are mingling, servers discretely bringing around hors d'oeuvres and flutes of champagne on trays. Farrah takes a glass, but I know she won't have so much as a sip. She's strict about not having alcohol or sugar.

Dalton is talking to June Calloway, giving her that same *boy next door* grin he tried on me earlier. She's eating it up, fluttering her lashes as she looks up at him and laughs.

I can still roll my eyes. That's silent. I see men like Dalton trying to get with Farrah all the time. They expect women to fall at their feet just because they're successful and attractive.

Which...in fairness, is more than any of the men I've gone out with have had to offer. It's been years since I've been on a date. But when I did date, I liked quirky, sweet men.

I've only had one serious relationship, and it started my freshman year of college. We'd been together for almost a year when he called me one night asking me to bail him out of jail. He had stolen several bottles of cologne. I broke things off with him after that, and of course, he never paid me back the bail money.

I don't miss having a partner. There was never anything grand or romantic about my relationship with Derek. We were more like good friends who also had sex.

I'm not a woman men look at like they do Farrah. Sometimes I see the heat and longing in their gazes when they look at her. I wonder what it would feel like if a man looked at *me* that way, like he was starving and nothing but me could satisfy him.

"I do. I love football," I overhear Farrah saying to JP. "You were on my last fantasy team, actually."

He laughs, looking pleased. She had no idea what fantasy football was until I explained it to her, and she's definitely never had her own team. I told her he'd be flattered if she said that, and it looks like I was right.

"Hope I did well for you," he says, his dimple showing when he smiles.

She does the coy, slow blink, with a one-second glance away that makes men forget they ever had common sense. When Farrah wants someone, she always gets them.

"You did great," she says with a wide, perfect smile. "Some of my others...well, it was a frustrating season."

"You just need an entire team of me," he quips.

"I wouldn't complain about that."

JP edges closer to her, a fish who has bitten the hook and is about to be reeled in. "So, where are you originally from, Farrah?"

"I grew up in a small town. Pella, Iowa. I still love to go back when I can for the tulip festival."

"Tulips, huh?"

"What can I say? We Dutch girls love our tulips." She brushes her fingers over his forearm and laughs lightly. "What about you--where did you grow up?"

"My family is originally from St. Louis, but we moved to Atlanta when I was in sixth grade so I'd have the best shot at a football scholarship."

From everything Farrah and I read about JP, he's one of the good ones. He started a charity to raise money for families who need help making their homes accessible for a family member with a disability. JP is considered one of the hottest, most eligible bachelors in pro sports, but he's selective about who he dates. He hasn't had a girlfriend for more than a year.

"Farrah, I'm Dalton Lorenzo."

The aggravated nose exhale from someone sitting near me is almost inaudible. Dalton buttoned his Hawaiian shirt up, losing most of his porn star cred. Farrah turns her megawatt smile his way.

"Hi Dalton, I'm Farrah." She shakes his hand and then pretends to sip her champagne. "So we have a hockey player and a football player. Is there a rivalry between those sports?"

"Nah," Dalton says. "We leave those guys to play with their balls."

JP shakes his head and smiles good-naturedly. "At least I still have all my teeth."

"I've only got one crown," Dalton says, pointing at one of his teeth. "And I didn't even chip that tooth playing hockey."

"How'd you chip it?" JP asks.

"Boxing."

JP lowers his brows. "Ooh, ouch. You don't

have enough extra brain cells to be boxing, Lorenzo."

June comes over to join the group, gushing to Farrah about the cosmetics line Farrah is working on. I stifle a yawn. It's been a long day of travel. As soon as filming wraps for the day, I have to get Farrah's ice bath ready for her face and do some prep for tomorrow.

I glance at my phone screen, seeing a text back from my mom.

*Mom: He's having a good day. Therapy went well. Hope Malibu is sunny and beautiful!*

The text makes me smile because I can picture her sitting at the little round oak kitchen table of the ranch house where I grew up in Newton, Kansas, as she wrote it. The white porcelain salt and pepper shakers passed down to her from her own mom always sit on a round tray in the center of the table, along with a stack of napkins.

The show's director, Alan, films the cocktail party for more than four hours, making some people pretend to meet for the first time several times so he'll have options to choose from for footage. Some of the contestants are more than a little tipsy by the time Alan finally calls it a night.

I'm relieved. It's one thing to watch Farrah

filming a movie, which is obviously fiction. All this fake chemistry seems pointless to me.

I slip away as soon as I can, knowing Farrah will want her facial ice bath as soon as she gets to her room.

"DID YOU THINK HE WAS REALLY INTERESTED IN ME, though? Like seriously interested?"

Farrah leans back from her spot in front of the sink in her bedroom's bathroom, her brows hiked up in question. I smile wearily.

"Of course he's interested."

"Don't do that thing where you just tell me all men are interested in me. You know what I'm asking."

"JP was practically drooling over you. He couldn't look away from you, even when you were walking away or talking to someone else. He is definitely very interested in you."

She walks into the bedroom, rubbing cleansing cream into her face. Her hair is pulled back with a terry cloth headband for her nighttime skin routine.

"I like him, too. He might be the one, Al. Isn't that crazy exciting?"

I know better than to tell her you can't choose a life partner based on meeting him at a cocktail party for a reality show. When Farrah sets her mind on something, she can't be reasoned with. She pays me to agree with her, so I do.

"So exciting." I feign enthusiasm.

"Did my eyes look puffy tonight?"

"No."

She gives me a stern look. "Are you lying? You can tell me the truth."

The truth is that I'm exhausted and sore from being run down by a pro hockey player today, but I can't say that.

"I'd tell you if your eyes looked puffy."

She walks back into the bathroom to rinse her face, returning to the bedroom about a minute later with an electric toothbrush in her mouth. She keeps talking, her words a jumble.

"I can't understand you."

She pulls the toothbrush out. "I said JP and Dalton are doing meditation and yoga with us tomorrow. On the beach."

Ugh. That sounds awful. More jokes about balls and competing to make Farrah laugh.

"I think it should just be you and them," I suggest. "Much more intimate."

She glares at me. "No. I'm not trying to have a threesome or anything. I need you to gauge everything for me, Al. You're my gauge."

"Okay, I'll be there."

"Meditation and yoga are so good for you. I keep waiting for you to love it as much as I do."

"Well...I don't *hate* it."

I do hate it. My mind won't turn off when we meditate. I run through a mental list of all the things I need to get done while trying to look like my mind is completely empty.

"Do you want to just stay in my room until things heat up with JP?" she asks.

God no. Farrah can run well on about five hours of sleep, but I can't. When we share a bed, she talks--and expects me to listen--until I'm fighting to stay awake. And even then, she keeps talking.

"All my stuff is in my room. I'll just sleep there."

She pouts for a second, then rebounds. "Okay, let's meet in the kitchen at six."

"Okay. Good night."

"Night, Al."

*four*

## DALTON

Malibu is different from Minneapolis in every way. The sun is just starting to rise and it's already warm here. I'm walking to the beach, sand slipping into my sandals and the smell of salt water filling the air.

It's not just the weather that's different. When I went out to grab a turkey wrap yesterday after filming, the guy behind the register at the deli glared at me when I pushed the button to tip twenty percent. Back home, people at restaurant counters apologize for the tipping option coming up automatically and tell me to just bypass it.

I wasn't happy when I found out I was being traded to the Mammoths. Minnesota felt boring compared to pro hockey cities like Chicago and New York. It's grown on me, though. I especially like summers, when everything is green, but it's still not brutally hot.

There are three silhouetted figures on the beach. The tall, broad one is JP, who's stretching out his hamstrings. Farrah is reaching both arms up in a stretch and Alice is standing off to the side.

"Hey, man," JP says as I approach them. "We were just talking about your sister surviving that plane crash with one of your teammates. I'd forgotten about it."

I slip my slides off, the sand massaging my soles. "Yeah, it was all over the news when it happened. Pretty crazy."

"Didn't she and your teammate get married after that?" Farrah asks.

"Yep."

"Were they dating before?"

"Nope."

Farrah inhales sharply and grins. "Oh, so did he put the moves on in the wilderness?"

Aggravation flares in my chest because even

though Trinity and Lincoln are happily married now, I still don't like thinking about them hooking up. Ever.

"It was a cabin in the woods."

"Oh." Farrah's eyes light happily. "That's romantic."

I walk over to Alice, eager to drop the subject. She gives me a skeptical look.

"Hey, how's your knee?"

"It's fine."

"Is it really?"

She shrugs. "Don't worry about it."

I sigh inwardly and turn to Farrah. "Did Alice tell you I accidentally clotheslined her yesterday and smashed your sushi?"

Farrah laughs lightly. "Is that what happened?"

"Dude, you boarded her without the boards," JP says.

I shoot him a glare. "I didn't know she was there. If you had better aim, I wouldn't have been running backward."

He scoffs. "I can put a football wherever I want. I just didn't realize you're so slow."

I give Alice a, *Can you believe this shit?* look, but she's stone-faced.

"Let's race," I suggest to JP.

The sand will slow me down a lot, but it'll slow him down, too. I've trained my legs hard over the years because speed is everything in hockey. There's not a doubt in my mind I can smoke him.

"I would, but my meniscus isn't all the way healed yet."

"Sorry, what?" I cup a hand around my ear like I didn't hear him. "Did you say you're too much of a puss?"

"Shit." He laughs. "I can't blow out my knee again, Lorenzo, or I'd take you on in a second."

"Boys." Farrah looks between us, a playful smile on her lips. "The vibe at morning meditation is zen. Peace. Let's get started."

She sits down in the sand, closing her eyes and straightening her spine. Then she leans forward, easily grasping her toes in a stretch. The rest of us follow her.

"Let's manifest health," she says in a soothing voice. "Wellness takes discipline. Let's think about all the actions we can take today to create wellness in our lives."

She leads us through a series of stretches, the sun popping up over the horizon within a few minutes. Farrah is all in with every movement; her flexibility amazing me. Her body is long and lean, her arm muscles defined when she gets into the plank position.

Alice follows in silence. She doesn't seem to have Farrah's enthusiasm for yoga. And JP is fucking obnoxious, vocally exhaling and making sure every movement is perfect.

I've got nothing against yoga--I do it several times a week. But that's because our team trainer makes us do it. Yoga with beautiful women, though, is much better than yoga with my teammates. Dane farts at least three times in every session.

"Dancer pose," Farrah murmurs.

She bends a knee behind her and turns toward it, grabbing her foot with her hand and bringing it up. My brows shoot up as I watch her move her foot above her head, holding it with both hands as she pushes her chest forward in a deep stretch.

"Alice will show you the modification," Farrah says in a tranquil tone.

Alice is bent forward, her leg out behind her. She puts her arms out, trying to balance, but flails and puts a hand down to the sand. She groans, frustrated.

"Progress, not perfection," Farrah says.

I look over at JP. He's damn close to getting into the pose, but he can't get his leg high enough. The strain is showing on his face, though he's trying to make it look like it's easy.

I've got the balance and core strength for this one. I get into the pose, feeling the deep stretch in my leg.

"Nice, Dalton," Farrah says. "Let's hold this one. Our bodies are so amazing, aren't they? We need to take care of them. Give our bodies the nutrients and oxygen they need. No processed garbage in."

Okay, that's where I draw the line. I have to stay fit for my job, and I'd exercise even if I didn't have to because I feel better when I do. But I also love pizza, candy bars and cheesesteak sandwiches.

"Are you vegan, Farrah?" JP asks.

"Pescatarian. But I don't eat much fish. What about you?"

"I have to get in a lot of calories, but I mostly eat lean proteins, whole grains and vegetables."

"Are you pescatarian, too, Alice?" I ask.

"Me?" She laughs and a little snort comes out. "No."

"But I'm working on her!" Farrah grins in Alice's direction.

Alice shakes her head. "I'll never give up bacon. Or chai tea lattes. Or pepperoni pizza."

"I could go for some pepperoni pizza," I say.

Farrah gasps. "Oh my God, stop it. Do you know how horrible pepperoni is? It has nitrates, high sodium and high saturated fats." She doesn't allow anyone a chance to respond before moving on. "Let's get into peacock pose. It'll be harder in the sand, but we can still do it."

Alice lets out a sigh that's almost inaudible. She just gets into a low plank, not even attempting peacock pose.

I know this one, and it's hard as hell to hold. It's similar to a handstand, but your forearms are on the ground and your body is at an angle instead of straight up.

JP admires Farrah as she gets into the pose, an appreciative smile tilting up the corners of his mouth. She has an amazing body, but I'm not openly ogling her the way he is.

I'm getting into peacock pose. I start in a low plank, then use my core to lift my lower body. My hands sink into the sand and I have to push myself up farther to keep my face out of the sand.

"Damn," JP mumbles. "This is no joke."

"You got it?" Farrah asks him.

"Yeah." His voice strains and he makes a spitting sound. "There's sand in my mouth, though."

"It's worth it! Our bodies were made for greatness. We're capable of so much more than we realize."

My glutes burn with the strain of holding peacock pose. Damn, I'm going to be sore after this. I've been taking it easy in the offseason, just doing a light run several days a week.

"Alice, try!" Farrah says.

"Nope, I'm good."

"You can't grow if you don't try."

"I don't want to grow."

Alice's cheekiness makes me smile. It's clear she doesn't want to be here. I bet Farrah makes her come. But I guess if Farrah wants part of Alice's workday to include yoga and meditation, that's between them.

"Let's challenge ourselves with handstand scorpion," Farrah says, bringing her feet back down to the ground.

Alice drops her knees to the sand, keeping the front of her body in the plank position.

"Al, at least try!" Farrah scolds.

"Nope. I'll injure myself."

"I can guide you."

Alice rolls her eyes. "That position is insane. I'm not doing it."

Farrah sighs. "Fine. But this one really helps keep you limbered up for...activities."

Her tone is mischievous. As JP and I watch, she gets into downward dog, moves her shoulders over her legs and lifts her legs--together--from the sand. It takes some time for her to stay balanced enough to get into a handstand position, but with her forearms flat on the ground. Then, she keeps moving her legs slowly until they're curved. She lowers her toes until they touch her hair.

"Holy..." JP murmurs.

He's right. It's fucking crazy. Farrah is trying to prove she can bend in any direction, and I think we know why. She looks like a Cirque do Soleil performer, her gaze serene.

"I'm not trying that," I say. "No way, man."

"Yeah, I'm out, too," JP says.

Farrah holds the pose, showing off at this point. Finally, she kicks her legs back into a handstand and lets them fall back to the ground.

"You're a dancer," JP says, a note of admiration in his tone.

She grins, clearly pleased. "I was a long time ago. Should we try sleeping yogi?"

SLEEPING YOGI TURNED OUT TO BE RIDICULOUS, too, unless you have a body without bones. By the time Farrah finishes the yoga session, we're all sweating heavily. It's not only the exertion but also the humidity.

"Let's take a quick break before the workout," Farrah says.

We walk up to the beach house, all of us taking a seat at a patio table.

"I could go for a swim." I eye the pool, an enormous rectangle shape with rocks, a waterfall and two hot tubs.

"Ugh, the chlorine would ruin my hair," Farrah says.

She looks over at Alice. "Can I get lavender water? And I'm craving cantaloupe. But only if it's super ripe."

"Sure."

I lower my brows, watching as Alice gets up

from her chair. Did Farrah just ask Alice to fetch her a water, like Alice is a dog?

"I'll grab you a water," I offer, getting up.

Farrah waves a hand. "No, let Alice do it. She knows how I like it."

I remember the bag of Voss water Alice was carrying, and the lemons and lavender. Surely Farrah isn't this much of a diva.

"Well, the chef is serving a big breakfast at seven thirty," I say. "I bet there'll be some fruit."

"Alice can run and get it. She's my assistant." She looks between me and JP. "Do you guys want water?"

Like hell is anyone bringing me a bottle of water instead of me walking into the house to get one myself. JP looks equally uncomfortable about it.

"I think I'm gonna go shower," I say. "See you guys at breakfast."

Alice had a long day yesterday, and her knee is hurt. But Farrah thought nothing of making her get up at dawn for yoga even though she didn't want to do it, and now she's making her wait on her.

I follow Alice to the kitchen.

"Hey," I say as I walk into the room. "You want me to bring her the water?"

She gives me a confused look. "No, I've got it."

I nod, still unsettled. "Is your knee okay? Is there anything I can do for you?"

She knits her brows together, a wrinkle forming between them. "No, I'm fine."

I want to say something else, but I'm starting to feel like a creep who won't leave her alone. So I shrug and leave the kitchen, going to my room for my shower.

*five*

## ALICE

WHY DO THEY CALL IT FAIR SKIN? BEING SO PALE and prone to burn within minutes of sun exposure is actually pretty *unfair*.

I'm wearing one of Farrah's wide-brimmed hats, sunglasses, a lightweight long-sleeved shirt and crop pants, but I still applied sunscreen. All my skin that was exposed yesterday is pink today, and I was hardly even outside.

Farrah, on the other hand, is golden, her skin glowing as she stands thigh-deep in the ocean. She's wearing the hell out of a black bikini, her blond hair blowing gently behind her in the breeze.

The producers are filming beach scenes today. They're pairing up contestants to take walks together, sit down in the sand and cool off in the water.

"I loved you in that space station movie," an up-and-coming politician, Josh Sellers, tells Farrah. "When you floated out of the air lock, I was like--is she done for?"

Farrah smiles. "That movie was so much fun to film. We got training from real astronauts."

Josh arches his brows, impressed. "No way. Did they give you any of their freeze-dried ice cream?"

"We did try some freeze-dried foods, but no ice cream."

She puts her feet on the ocean floor, standing up straight. She's just below knee-deep in the water. When she looks over at the director, Alan, he scrunches his face in aggravation.

"Cut!" he calls out.

"Alice, blot me," Farrah says.

I'm standing about ten feet behind the cameraman to be out of his way. I set down my bag and walk toward Farrah with one of the thin, paperlike sheets that absorb sweat, sliding out of my sandals before I enter the water.

"We have makeup people for that, and we don't break anytime you feel like it," Alan says.

Farrah gives him her trademark smile. "Alice knows how I want it done."

I blot her face and chest as quickly as I can, waves lapping against the bottom of my pants.

"This isn't a swimsuit cover shoot," Alan says. "I need continuous footage, and I have a full schedule today. No more stopping."

"I don't want to be dripping sweat on camera."

Alan pinches the bridge of his nose. "It's summer in California. Everyone is sweating." He gestures at the cameraman, still holding his heavy equipment in the air. "Danny sweated all the way through his T-shirt."

Farrah ignores him, looking at me instead.

"How's my hair?"

"It's good."

"Is this camera angle working, or--"

Alan throws the ink pen in his hand. It flies about ten feet before flopping to the sand unceremoniously.

"I decide the camera angles! Alice, I need you out of my shot right now."

It would be unusual for Farrah not to piss off

the director of whatever she's filming. But I hate being dragged into it.

I duck my head and walk back to my spot behind Danny. This time, I go farther, so I can take out my phone to check and see if my mom has texted me back.

*Mom: He wasn't up for his therapy today. He didn't sleep well last night.*

I hate that I can't be there. If Dad didn't sleep well last night, neither did Mom. She carries a lot of weight on her shoulders as his caregiver, and she never complains. My brother and I both wish she would, though. I worry she'll just implode one day, too exhausted and overwhelmed to keep doing what she does.

*Alice: Did he miss speech therapy? That one is really important to help with his chewing.*

*Mom: I know. But he refused to go. We are okay, honey. Are you enjoying California?*

I sigh softly. My mom is a *glass-all-the-way-full* person. She sees things from an overly positive perspective, and I know it's partially a protective mechanism for her because the truth can be heavy and scary when you're the long-term caregiver of a disabled person.

*Alice: It's very sunny here. I'll FaceTime you guys this evening.*

*Mom: We'd love that! Thanks for the picture of the beautiful sunrise! Your dad smiled when I showed it to him.*

I send a smile emoji and put my phone back in my bag, wishing I could talk to my brother Will. But he's in his first year of surgical residency in Chicago, and he doesn't get much downtime. We have a call scheduled for this weekend, so I'll have to wait until then.

Alan films Farrah and Josh for about ten more minutes. As soon as he's done, Farrah walks over to me.

"That guy's a bore," she says under her breath.

"Who, Alan?"

She laughs lightly. "Well, yeah. But I meant Josh."

I change the subject because Josh isn't that far away, and it feels rude to be talking about him when he could overhear. "Are you on a break?"

"Yep. I think I'll have scrambled egg whites for lunch."

That's a relief. I'd love to get out of the sun and get a respite from this hot hat.

"Sure. Anything else?"

"Mmm, I'll also take half a cucumber, sliced. And extra water."

"I'll have to go to the grocery store for the cucumber, which is fine because I also need to pick up some more collagen."

She furrows her brow. "I only like that one brand. The one you order online."

"Well, it's back-ordered. I can't get it right now."

She huffs out a sigh. "Why do businesses make it so hard to support them?"

I love Farrah, but a part of me wants to shake her and ask her if she has any idea how many people would love for their biggest problem to be using a new brand of collagen in their smoothies.

"But then I'll have to wait for the eggs," she muses. "Okay, so make the eggs and then go to the store and I'll have the cucumber as a snack."

"Okay."

"Did Lisa call about that contract?"

I take Farrah's phone out of my bag and check the screen to see if her agent called.

"Not yet."

"Call her office. I want that contract wrapped."

"I will."

She glances down at her chest and then back to me. "Are you sure my boobs look good in this top?"

"They look amazing," I assure her for the third time today.

She hesitates. "Okay."

Later that evening, I'm sitting alone on the beach, oblivious to the people who occasionally walk past me on their beach strolls. It's just after eight p.m. I had to fight Farrah to get out of dinner with the contestants.

As soon as I heard the chef's menu for tonight included pate and pureed beets, I told Farrah I was having dinner on my own. Normally, she likes to have me beside her for meals when she's working.

It's been a day, though. I was the go-between for Farrah and Lisa over the contract for Farrah's next film since Farrah was busy filming the show today and couldn't talk to Lisa herself. I also had to hit up multiple grocery stores to get all the Voss water I needed.

Then there's my dad. I just FaceTimed my parents and he didn't look like he was feeling well. He put on a brave face and communicated with me through the computer that's now his voice, but it was bittersweet. I haven't seen my parents since Christmas, almost six weeks ago. Even then, I only got two days off from Farrah. She gave me a big holiday bonus to make up for the lack of time off.

I miss watching Jeopardy with my dad and eating subs from my mom's favorite place with her while we play Scrabble.

With a heavy sigh, I take the double bacon cheeseburger from the white paper bag I picked up at a drive-through. I only had time to grab one pancake from the breakfast spread this morning, which I rolled up and ate without syrup. Instead of eating lunch, I was doing things for Farrah.

The cheeseburger smells like heaven as I unwrap it. A little grease drips onto my fingers. I sink my teeth into it for a huge bite, closing my eyes.

It tastes amazing. Eating this burger and drinking the strawberry shake I got with it is the first thing I've done just because I wanted to in a long time.

Filming today was pretty much just absurd. The contestants were directed to do things like flirt, give meaningful glances and touch affectionately.

It's all so fake. Even the parts of the show that are real are gross. Today, the rock star, Dom

Marone asked the Olympic gymnast Misty Meyers how much she weighs. She's way more muscular than he is. She smiled sweetly and said she'd tell him how much she weighs if he'd tell her how many times he's shot up or snorted the drugs that have left him borderline emaciated.

That's probably not making Alan's cut, but I thoroughly enjoyed it. Misty could kick Dom's ass, and I hope, at some point, she will.

"Hey, how's it going?"

I look up, my mouth full with a bite of my burger, and see Dalton standing there. He's wearing athletic shorts, an Ohio State T-shirt and a backward baseball cap.

I chew as quickly as I can, putting my hand over my mouth before I answer. "What's wrong? Does Farrah need something?"

He smiles. "Probably, but I'm not aware of anything."

"She didn't send you down here to get me?"

"Nope. I'm just walking on the beach. Everyone else is eating lemon sorbet."

I nod, sipping my milkshake.

"Looks like you were smarter than me," he says. "I had a little poof of meat mousse for dinner."

"Sounds filling."

"Do you mind if I sit?"

I shrug. "No, I don't mind."

He sits down beside me, putting his knees up and resting his forearms on them. For a minute, we sit in silence, the crashing waves the only sound. I catch a hint of his scent--a light, clean smell with a note of sandalwood.

"Been to Malibu before?" he asks.

"Farrah had an event here once. But I stayed at the hotel the entire time, so I don't think it counts."

He looks out at the darkened ocean water. "It's my first time. It's really different from Minneapolis."

"Is that where you grew up?"

"No, but it's home now. I grew up in Ohio. What about you?"

"Detroit, Michigan."

"I've got a buddy there. A friend from high school."

A couple walks in front of us, hand in hand. Once they're past, Dalton looks over at me. "So, how long have you worked for Farrah?"

"Let see...almost three years."

"Do you travel home for your time off?"

I smile wryly. "What time off?"

He pinches his brows together. "You do get time off, right?"

I subtly breathe a little deeper, wishing I could lean closer and smell him better. "I go home for Thanksgiving and Christmas."

He just looks at me in silence for a few seconds. "Are you serious? She won't give you time off?"

There's a flare of aggravation in my chest. "It's not that she won't. It's complicated."

"Were you exaggerating? You get weekends off, right?"

I almost laugh because I can't imagine what I'd do by myself for two full days. Before I worked for Farrah, I had two jobs. I haven't had two days in a row to do nothing in more than six years.

"Our setup works for us," I say, hoping he'll drop the subject.

"Are you happy working for her? Running errands and getting water and blotting her sweaty face?"

I am already emotional over my parents, and his completely out-of-line questions send me over the edge. I pick up my fast-food bag and stand up.

"Fuck off, Dalton. You don't know anything about me."

"Hey, I didn't mean to offend you. I just--"

"You don't have a fucking clue." I'm yelling at him now, the guy walking by with his dog veering out of the way to avoid us. "But how could you? You're a millionaire pro athlete starring on a reality TV show."

"Alice--"

I flip him off. "Thanks for ruining my few minutes of peace, asshole."

I turn and try to stomp off angrily, but my feet sink into the sand. Damn. Trying to storm away from this conversation is turning into a workout, my calves feeling it.

Dalton doesn't follow me to try to defend himself. Good move on his part.

I'm normally even-tempered. I have to be working for Farrah. But Dalton made his shitty comments on the wrong day. Angry tears fill my eyes as I walk around the house, avoiding the back entrances where I'll run into people.

Instead, I slip in through a side entrance and go to my room. Once there, I close the door and curl up on the bed, still crying.

Are these angry tears? They are, but they're sad, too. I picture my parents' faces on the call tonight, both of them looking older than I remembered. And tired. So tired.

Who am I to feel sorry for myself when my mom does what she does? I swipe the tears from my face and take a few deep breaths.

I take a minute to breathe before I pick up my phone to respond to the text Farrah just sent.

It was just a bad day. Tomorrow will be better.

six

## DALTON

THIS IS WHAT I GET FOR TRYING TO BE FRIENDLY. I put my foot in my mouth and now Alice is pissed at me. I'm already battling JP to get Farrah to pick me, and now her assistant thinks I'm a prick.

In fairness, I am a prick sometimes. If someone messes with one of my teammates on the ice, they don't have to worry about an enforcer coming for them--it'll be me. A good captain stands up for his teammates. Coaches have told me I stand up too much, especially at times when we can't afford penalty kills because I'm in the penalty box.

That's me, though. I don't wear my heart on my

59

sleeve, but when it comes to hockey, my fists are an effective way of letting people know how I'm feeling. I can also be impatient. When I was a rookie, I ran my mouth like it was my job. I've mellowed, but I'm still pretty set in my ways.

I wasn't being a prick to Alice, though. I was trying to be helpful. If she tells Farrah what I said, I'll have to figure out who my second choice is to end up with. Farrah will be all over JP, and that smug bastard will never let me live it down.

Dara Houser wouldn't be bad. She's a model who's famous because she has famous parents, but she's twenty-four. She does a weird, pouty thing with her lips all the time, but that's better than Cara's selfie obsession.

I lie back in the sand, putting my knees up as I look up at the bright stars in the night sky. I'm not ready to go back to the beach house. I don't want to run into Alice, and I'm tired of socializing with celebrities.

I don't think of myself as a celebrity. I'm just a hockey player, and that's more than enough for me. So far, Alice is the only person I've met here who seems down to earth.

I'm flipping through the new round of pictures

Trinity sent of my baby nephew Micah when I get a text.

*Rita: Did you get my voicemail? I'll be there tomorrow late morning.*

Fuck. The only Rita I know is Rita Kenney, the head of PR for the league. I push a button on my phone screen to listen to her voicemail.

"Dalton, Rita Kenney. The producers of the show are letting me come on set tomorrow with a photographer to get some content for socials. I'm bringing you some T-shirts and hats to wear with our logos. Give me a call back and let me know what size tumbler you'd like. I have twenty ounce, thirty-two ounce and forty-six ounce. They all have the logo for the foundation, but I don't have room in my suitcase for all of them. Call me back, thanks."

Grimacing, I sit up. I'm not getting paid extra for doing this show, and I'm not walking around in a league T-shirt and hat. Just the thought of Rita coming here puts me on edge.

Last season was my first as team captain, and it was rocky. Lincoln was our team captain, and he was great at it. He always knew what to say. When we got cocky as a team, he knocked us back down to earth. And when we were down, he built us back up.

Me? I fight our opponents. But leadership is more than that. I choked in the final game of the playoffs and we lost. Coming here was supposed to be a break for me. A way to recharge.

Now I'm going to have Rita up my ass. Hopefully it'll only be for a few hours.

I get up, brushing the sand off my clothes and out of my hair. Between pissing off Alice and finding out Rita's coming here, I need a drink.

"Better not be anything but water in there, Lorenzo." JP grins as he passes me coming out of the library the next afternoon, nodding toward my stainless tumbler.

"Unfortunately, there's not," I call after him.

The producers nixed Rita's idea to make me a walking commercial for the league, thank fuck. The hat she brought looked like it had been balled up in her bag, and it smelled like powder. I'm appeasing her by using the cup.

"There's our resident motherpucker," Alex

quips when he sees me. "Can you close the door, please?"

Rita, sitting in one of the library's plush wingback chairs, shoots him a shocked look.

"He better not be sleeping with the contestant who's a single mom. Or even trying to. I said that was a non-starter during the contract negotiations."

Alex waves a hand dismissively. "No, we've got someone else picked out for Hailey. That was just a bad joke on my part since he's a hockey player." He claps his hands together. "Have a seat, Dalton. I'm staying on schedule today if it kills me, so let's get started."

I sit in the chair next to Alex's. He has a habit of clicking the top of his pen on repeat, and he does it as he asks me, "How are you feeling about things so far, Dalton?"

I shrug. "Fine. We're just getting started, so I don't have much to base an opinion on."

Click. Click. Click. Click. Click. "Right, sure. So tonight, we'll be kicking things up a notch. The men will play a game of beach volleyball, four on four, and the winning four players each get to choose one woman to take out for a one-on-one date."

"How are you at beach volleyball?" Rita asks me.

Is she serious? I play fucking ice hockey and I live in Minneapolis. "Uh...it's been a while."

"With two pro athletes on the same volleyball team, I'm confident they'll have no trouble," Alex says.

"And who are the options for his date?" Rita asks.

"June would be my preference."

"No way. She's only twenty and she was arrested last year for disorderly conduct. The league doesn't want one of our players associated with her."

Click. Click. Alex considers. "Well, I wanted to wait longer to ramp up to you and JP both vying for Farrah, but if you get to pick before he does, you could go for her."

I open my mouth to respond, but Rita beats me to it. "How will you decide who picks first?"

"It'll all be worked out beforehand, and then we'll meet with those four men again before the selection ceremony to confirm we're all on the same page. In the event two players want to choose the same woman, we'll give first choice to whoever scored more points in the volleyball game."

I focus my gaze on the rows of hardback books lining the shelves of the open two-story library. Hockey seasons are long and grueling. How did I end up spending a big chunk of my short offseason on a reality show where I'm playing beach volleyball to compete over a date?

This would be a lot more fun if my teammates were here. Even one or two of them. I'm not used to being on my own this much without my trusted friends at my back. Even in our offseason, we still spend a lot of time together.

"If you can't get Farrah, you need to choose Misty," Rita says.

"I'll consider it."

She drops her brows, her mouth falling open. "Consider it? Dalton, you are a reflection of the league. You don't want to know how many hours I spent in meetings with the higher-ups, *begging* them to let me pick a player to be on this show. And I picked you. If you make the league look bad, it's my neck on the line. My job. I'm fifty-three years old, if I get fired--"

"Rita." I lean forward in my seat, resting my elbows on my knees. "I'm twenty-nine years old, which makes me an adult. I'm a representative of the league all the time, and I haven't blown it yet."

"Oh really? How about the viral video of you beating your stick against the ground in a rage after a loss?"

"That was more...passion than rage."

"This show is a huge opportunity for the league. I don't want you to just get through it without incident. I want you to become the most recognized player we have. The one people are rooting for to find love. We have to bring real numbers to the league to justify this. Higher social media views, higher merch sales--"

I look down at the ground and then back up at her. "I never agreed to any of that. I didn't ask you to risk your job for me."

"Okay, if I could just intervene," Alex says. "I think we're all on the same page here. Dalton, you like Farrah Reed, right? I mean, what straight man doesn't?"

"Yeah, I like her."

"Is there some other contestant you're burning for that I don't know about?"

"I don't know anyone very well yet, but...no."

He smiles and puts his hands out. "Then we're okay! Rita, Farrah is your first choice for Dalton, right?"

"Absolutely."

"Then let's move ahead as planned. Rita, you can come by anytime or reach out to my assistant for updates. This is my fifth season doing this show, and I know what works. We need viewers to stay hooked, and that requires some drama. But this is all gonna pan out just fine." He looks at his wristwatch. "I have to go. Dalton, get practicing those volleyball serves!"

It's not a bad idea. And it will get me away from Rita. I excuse myself, planning to find JP and get in some practice since I know we'll be on the same team.

I'm also hoping to run into Alice so I can apologize for last night. She wouldn't even look at me during the yoga session this morning.

Farrah still seems interested in both me and JP, though, so I don't think Alice told her what I said. I just hope she doesn't decide to.

## seven

ALICE

*HOURS.* I'M GOING TO HAVE SEVERAL HOURS TO myself while Farrah is on her date with Dalton. After the day I've had, I kind of want to spend it in bed staring at the ceiling and not thinking about anything. But this is too precious an opportunity to waste.

There was a sand volleyball game last night, and Dalton and JP dominated. They scored almost every point their team got, Dalton edging JP out with two more points. That meant Dalton got first choice for a one-on-one date tonight, and he picked Farrah.

After seeing his display of aggressive athleticism, not to mention his washboard abs, she was excited about the date. She wore a red dress cut so low it leaves nothing to the imagination, and she looks incredible in it.

I'm sure Dalton "the douchebag" Lorenzo won't tell her he thinks she needs to get her own water from the fridge, but who cares? I'm freaking alone, and it's not time to crawl into bed and hope I can get some good sleep before the alarm goes off for yoga while it's still dark outside.

Dalton has been giving me puppy dog eyes and I can tell he wants to apologize for his douchery, but I'm evading him because I don't want to hear it. While Farrah lay out by the pool today, I was hand-washing her lingerie. Scoping out the restaurant she and Dalton would be at tonight because she wanted to make sure the lighting and camera angles would be flattering. And reviewing her strict dietary restrictions with the restaurant's chef so she could breezily order dinner without sounding high maintenance.

That went great. The chef doesn't use ceramic cookware, which Farrah insists on, so I had to go buy him a saucepan and convince him to use it to cook her meal tonight. He called me a few choice names, so I had to break out my cash stash and buy his compliance.

When I finally got back to the house, Farrah's organic, plant-based lunch in hand, she said she fell asleep in the lounge chair and had a dream that would be a great movie plotline. She insisted on telling me about it while I took notes on my laptop so I could write up a proposal for a studio.

The chef at the house is making brick-oven pizzas to order tonight. My stomach growls angrily as I walk into the kitchen because I haven't had time to eat today.

A chef's assistant, Carly, sees me and smiles, going over to a stack of white boxes and taking off the one on top.

"Perfect timing. I just took yours out of the oven. One pizza with garlic, extra cheese and extra pepperoni."

The heavenly scents of pepperoni and roasted garlic make my mouth water with anticipation. My eyes fill with tears as I take the box from Carly.

"Thank you for this. It's been a day, and...just thank you. I really appreciate it."

"We've got you, girl. Go relax and enjoy it.

There's red wine, water, tea and lemonade on the sideboard in the main dining room."

I take a cleansing breath as I walk away, embarrassed that I almost cried over a damn pizza. My emotions must be running high. They definitely were when I unleashed my fury on Dalton.

My job is none of his business, and he really should have just kept on walking instead of sitting down to chat with me. But I may have taken some other things out on him, and that may not have been fair.

That's an issue for Tomorrow Alice, because Today Alice has fucking had it and she deserves a big glass of wine and some pizza.

I avoid eye contact with everyone I pass as I go to the dining room to get some wine because I'm so hungry I can only think about the first bite of this pizza that smells life changing.

Fortunately, no one even tries to look at me. Everyone in the house stops Farrah or says something to her when they see her, but most of them don't even know my name. They just call me "Farrah's assistant" and mostly ignore me.

I'm able to make my way out to the beach, where I settle beneath an umbrella that Misty was using earlier. Sand makes a killer cup holder for my wineglass. It's just me, the sparkling ocean near sunset, and my dinner.

The pizza is incredible. I savor every bite, eating six of the eight slices. The chef couldn't have chosen a better night for pizzas, not just because I may have an orgasm from eating mine but also because Farrah wouldn't have eaten this. I would've spent my evening getting her dinner. So I guess I kind of owe Dalton for picking her for his date.

Maybe she'll come out of this show in a relationship. That would be great for me. When she's dating someone, I get breaks from her when she's on dates. The overnight ones are my favorite because I get to skip sunrise yoga and workout. But it's been a while since she's had a boyfriend.

An occasional date so she can be photographed and make headlines? Yes. But someone meeting her crazy high standards and making it to relationship status? Not so much.

When I'm done with dinner, I take out my phone, willing it to not have a text from Farrah.

No such luck.

*Farrah: Dalton smells good. It's making me horny.*
*Farrah: God I want a margarita. Must stay strong!*

*Farrah: Okay, if Dalton and I don't report for yoga in the morning, don't come to my room looking for me...*

*Farrah: But don't miss yoga because I'll wake up no matter how late we're up.*

I text back a quick *okay and good luck*, and then take a chance and call my brother, planning to leave him a long check-in voicemail.

"Hey, Alice," he says.

I smile, the sound of his voice reminding me of home. "Wow, you answered. Are you on a break from saving people?"

"I just got off a fifteen-hour shift. I'm walking to the train. It's good to hear your voice. How are you?"

I sigh softly. "Kind of wishing we'd been born identical twins instead of fraternal so we could swap places. You would've scrubbed the crotch of another person's undies with your hands today and been called a provincial fucking fool by a French chef."

"Okay, not ideal. But you would have removed a screwdriver handle from a guy's ass, so..."

I laugh. "Stop it, you did not."

"Oh, I did. And two pairs of rubber gloves didn't feel like enough for that job."

"First of all, how?"

"You mean, how'd it happen, or how'd I get it out?"

"I can imagine how it happened to him. He was getting railed with a screwdriver and it broke off."

"He tried to tell us he didn't know how it got in there. When the nurse told him we had to call the police because it sounded like he'd been assaulted, he owned it."

I close my eyes, laughing softly. "Oh my God, the absolute mortification."

"Yeah. My attending was like, *This is all you, Morrow.*"

"So how did you get it out?"

"Rectal retractor and my hand. I did not get paid enough today. I promise you that."

I feel more relaxed than I have since arriving at the beach house. Talking to Will has that effect on me.

"Well, you win. Your day was worse than mine."

"Why the hell are you washing Farrah's underwear by hand?"

"I always have. She prefers her lingerie be hand-washed."

He scoffs. "Well, fuck. Can't a Laundromat do that?"

"Nope. Do you know what some people would

be capable of if they knew they had Farrah Reed's worn underwear?"

"Jesus. That's...disgusting but completely true."

"How are you, seriously? Are you holding up okay?"

"Yeah, I'm good. The hours are long, but I love it. I'm hoping to get home next weekend to see Mom and Dad."

A passerby nods as she walks past me with two big German shepherds. I smile, wishing I could pet the dogs.

"Good. I FaceTimed them the other night, and I thought Dad seemed more tired than usual. And Mom said he refused his therapies two different days. I'm worried."

Will pauses before saying, "So am I."

I sit up straighter. "You are? Why?"

"I should have texted you. Mom called me last week because Dad's been really fatigued and his urine output has decreased."

My heart pounds nervously. Why didn't my mom tell me any of this?

"Okay. Is it some kind of nutritional deficiency? I can overnight a supplement to them. Why didn't Mom--"

"I wish it were something like that. The medication he's on to prevent more strokes can cause kidney issues for people who are on it long term."

I'm quiet as I consider my brother's words. He isn't offering up a solution, and I don't like that.

"What does that mean, Will? And don't bullshit me."

"I mean, I haven't seen him recently, so it's hard for me to say for sure. I told her to get him in with a nephrologist, but she can't find anyone in their network who has an opening less than three months out."

"I'll pay for it. Wherever he can get in, I'll pay for it."

"You're already spending a lot on their expenses and in-home help. And we're not just talking about one consultation. There'll be tests and probably treatment."

Panic rises in my throat, clawing at my ability to breathe. "I have forty-two thousand dollars, Will. And you know how much Farrah pays me. If I can get a payment plan--"

He cuts me off. "It's been six years, Alice. He's beaten the odds just by staying alive this long."

"I'll ask Farrah to call in a favor. She knows people."

"Listen to me." Will's stern tone takes me by surprise. "If I think he needs it when I get there this weekend, I'll make sure he gets admitted to a hospital. I'm getting him in with a specialist here within the next two weeks. We'll know more then."

I squeeze my eyes shut, admitting something I can only say out loud to my brother. "I'm scared."

"Yeah, me too. But I'm not a nephrologist, and neither are you. Let's wait until we get more information, okay?"

"Yeah."

"You doing okay?"

I can barely hear him over the background noise. "What?"

"It's the train. I'll talk to you later, okay?"

"Okay. Love you."

"Love you, too."

I end the call, my tears blurring the oranges and pinks of the sky as the sun slips past the horizon for the night. My chest aches with worry.

My brother is the smartest person I've ever known. He's a doctor. Even though he's still completing his education, he sent me a picture of his white coat and it has "Dr. William Morrow" stitched on it.

As hard as it is, I have to do what he says and wait until we know more about what's going on with our dad. Even if it's hell to be waiting at a massive pink Malibu beach house while a reality show is filmed around me.

*eight*

## DALTON

"Push that chest out and inhale the ocean air," Farrah instructs. "Let your core show you how much it can do for you."

It's the morning after our one-on-one date, and I'm tired but felt like I needed to be here anyway. Now that I've been here several mornings in a row, it would look bad if I just quit coming. And this is my chance to get Alice alone and apologize.

The date with Farrah last night was...fine. I can't think of any other word for it. She's incredibly beautiful; no one can deny that. But she talked about herself for two hours at dinner and for two more when we went bowling.

The producers rented out the entire bowling alley for our date, and when the woman who worked there started crying over meeting Farrah, Farrah was great about it. She hugged her and posed for pictures. But when the woman was telling Farrah how much one of her movies means to her because she and her mom watched it together while her mom was terminally ill, Farrah cut her off.

She said, "Aw, I love that." And she didn't let the woman finish what she was saying. I saw the flicker of disappointment on the woman's face when Farrah interrupted her, said she loved it and then walked away.

I can't stop thinking about it. I might not have cared about something like that at age twenty. I hope I would've, but I was different then. At twenty-nine, I'm wiser. My mom had a breast cancer scare a few years ago. I thought I lost my sister in a plane crash. I've seen how much it means to terminally ill kids to meet their athlete heroes.

That woman was shaking with excitement, and Farrah wasn't even truly listening to her. She wasn't listening to me, either, the few times I was able to get a word in edgewise on our date.

I played it off. Smiled and showed interest until the very end, when she kissed me outside her bedroom door. I could tell she was going to invite me into her room, so I said good night and left.

"Hold it," Farrah calls out. "Come on, guys, you can do it!"

We've been in a side plank position for a solid three minutes. I glance over at Alice. Her hand that's in the air--pointing toward the sky as she holds the side plank--is flipping the bird.

It makes me smile. Alice tries to be plain wallpaper, just blending into the background and not really being noticed, but she's got personality, and she's anything but boring.

"Okay, good."

Farrah moves her arm down and Alice lets herself collapse onto the sand, chest down, with a groan.

"Your body is thanking you, Al," Farrah says.

"Yeah, right. Eat shit, body."

"Hey guys, sorry I'm late." JP approaches us, shirtless.

His athletic shorts hang down on his hips. I want to make a quip about him stepping up his game, but I don't. He was pissed I outplayed him at sand volleyball and got the date with Farrah. He ended up on a date with Melanie Tillman, a contestant who's a self-made billionaire businesswoman.

I'm guessing he had a better evening than I did. But then again, his bare chest tells me he's competing harder than ever for Farrah.

Whatever. It hasn't even been a week and I'm already over this show. We all have to go on a sunset cruise tonight, but what I really want is a break from the damn cameras. They're always there, from eight a.m. on.

Farrah leads us the rest of the way through yoga, giving me a few flirty smiles. I'm relieved when she finally says we're done.

"Ten-minute break before the workout?" she says.

Alice is already walking back toward the house. She skips the workouts, instead using that time to prepare Farrah's lemon lavender water for the day and straighten up Farrah's bedroom.

"Hey, no workout for me today," I tell Farrah. "Okay if I steal Alice for a little bit?"

She arches her brows and smiles. "Is someone trying to find out all my deepest secrets from my assistant?"

I grin, not missing a beat. "You caught me."

Alice is still walking away. Farrah calls after her.

"Al, Dalton wants to talk to you."

Alice heard me. She just doesn't care. It was kind of a dick move getting Farrah to make her talk to me, but otherwise, Alice wouldn't have wanted to. She also wouldn't have time because she's busy every minute with Farrah's shit.

When Alice turns around, her expression is a combination of annoyance and resignation.

"Let's walk," I say because I don't want to have to talk to her in the kitchen while she's working.

She's carrying her slides, because we all do yoga in bare feet. With a slight sinking of her shoulders, she walks toward me.

"Don't tell him about Bali, Al!" Farrah says. "What happens in Bali stays in Bali."

Alice gives her a broad smile that disappears as soon as she turns around.

"I don't give a fuck what happened in Bali," I say under my breath.

That gets me a hint of a smile. I'll take it.

I lead her away from JP and Farrah, heading down the side of the beach that leads to a huge wood pier about a mile away.

"She loves pink roses," Alice says. "Her favorite color is purple and she likes to sniff freshly unwrapped Kit Kat bars, but she won't eat them. She sometimes licks them, but she feels guilty about it."

I furrow my brow because the Kit Kat thing tracks, but it's still fucking ridiculous.

"That's not what I want."

She looks confused for a second, but then realization dawns. "Oh, you don't need to apologize over the other night, Dalton. I was upset about something else and I took it out on you."

"It doesn't matter. I was still out of line, and I'm sorry."

"It's okay."

I shake my head. "I'm used to letting shit fly out of my mouth because I do that with my teammates. And I meant what I said to you, but it wasn't my business."

I'm sweaty from yoga, so I walk into the water, letting it lap around my ankles as we walk. Alice is quiet for a couple of minutes before she responds.

"I know how it seems. Farrah's...just Farrah, and some of the stuff I have to do for her is ridiculous."

"I'm glad we agree on that."

She looks over and up at me, her expression earnest. "But."

"Damn. This is where we're gonna part ways, isn't it? Where you try to tell me why you shouldn't get weekends off? Because other assistants can't step in and take over for you?"

She sighs, her gaze locked onto the pier. "My dad owned his own electrician business in Detroit. My mom stayed at home with me and my brother until we were in high school, and then she got a job as a receptionist at a veterinarian's office. My brother and I started college and everything was good until six years ago when my dad had a stroke."

The sadness in her voice hits me right in the chest. "I'm so sorry, Alice."

"He couldn't work anymore. My mom had to quit her job to take care of him. My brother and I were nineteen."

"You're a twin?"

She smiles. "I am. My brother's name is Will. And he's so smart. So fucking smart and hardworking. He was going to school on a full scholarship, and I was a psychology major with no scholarships and not a ton of interest in psychology, just going because my parents were adamant that their kids finish school. So it was an easy decision. I quit school and made Will stay in."

I stop walking. "You quit school?"

"I had to. My parents had no income. They would've lost their house. So I moved back home and started working two jobs."

I'm so wrapped up in her story that even though I don't want to interrupt her, I want to know everything.

"What were the jobs?"

"By day, I worked at a printing place, and by night, I was a server at a steak house."

"Wow. Like how many hours a week are we talking?"

She considers. "Thirty-seven hours at the print shop because they had to pay benefits for full-time people, and usually thirty-five at the steak house."

She starts walking again, and I follow, the breeze blowing the dark waves of her hair in all directions.

"I made sixty-seven thousand dollars a year between both jobs. It was such a fucking struggle to keep the house and have food on the table. We couldn't pay the medical bills. My parents hated that I'd quit school to support them."

I imagine nineteen-year-old Alice carrying all this weight on her shoulders and doing it willingly. Gladly. I was a playboy pro hockey player at nineteen, and I didn't have to take care of anyone but myself.

"So my mom had a friend from college who worked for a Hollywood agent," she continues. "She found out about an actress who needed a very reliable, trustworthy assistant, and she recommended me. It was a lot more money, but it was a very hard decision because it meant I couldn't be with my parents anymore. I couldn't help with my dad's care. I had to make a hard decision. Either bust my ass to *not* cover all the bills but be there to help. Or move away for about twice as much money as I was making."

I shake my head. "That had to be hard."

"It was the hardest thing I've ever done." Her voice breaks with emotion and she turns away. "I went, obviously."

I stop and move in front of her, putting my hands on her shoulders. "Hey."

She takes a step back, looking over her shoulder. "Don't. She thinks we're talking about her."

I look down the beach to where Farrah and JP had been. They're gone.

"She's not there."

Alice looks at the house. "She still might be able to see us. We should keep walking."

She swipes her fingertips over her cheeks. "So I was Farrah's primary assistant, and I did get weekends off. Not that I knew anyone in LA or had anything to do. But she didn't like the other assistants, so she offered me more money to be her around-the-clock person."

I blow out a breath. "I've never felt like a bigger asshole than I do right now."

"You didn't know."

Her eyes shine with unshed tears. "That money has changed my family's lives. My dad's bills are current. We can get him all the therapies he needs, and there are so many. He has a wheelchair that makes his life and my mom's life better. A wheelchair-accessible van."

She fetches Farrah's waters and buys her Kit Kats to sniff so she can help her family. That's why it's never too much. Why she doesn't care about not having time off.

I stop walking again. She looks at me, her brows lowered in confusion.

"I'm hugging you now, and I don't give a fuck who sees," I say.

Her eyes widen with alarm. I wrap my arms around her waist and hug her with my whole body, pulling her against me. She's stiff at first, but then she relaxes against me, her breath dancing across my throat as she sighs softly.

"You're incredible."

"I didn't tell you all that so you'd think--"

"Stop it. You're an incredible person, Alice. It means a lot that you trusted me with all that."

She sniffles. "If you knew my parents, you'd know..." She clears her throat. "They're the incredible ones."

I close my eyes, emotion welling in my throat. She relaxes another degree, letting me really hold her. We stand like that for a long time, the ocean's waves and her softness bringing a peaceful feeling I don't want to let go of.

When she pulls away, I immediately miss her warmth against me.

"Please don't tell anyone," she says pleadingly. "Farrah doesn't know."

I scoff. "Of course not. She's only interested in herself."

Alice pinches her brows together. "I don't even know why I told you all that. I guess because I'm worried about my dad. And I miss my family."

"I'm glad you did. And I'm sorry you can't be with them."

Her lips curve up in a smile. "Thank you.

You're ruining my asshole perception of you, by the way."

I laugh. "Well, it's gonna be utterly shattered when I tell you this next thing."

She nods, telling me to get on with it. "You're not an actor, no need for dramatic pauses."

I laugh again, and this time, it's a full-throated, truly amused one. "Alice, if I could take any woman here out for a date tonight, it'd absolutely be you."

*nine*

## ALICE

*IT'D ABSOLUTELY BE YOU.*

I can't stop replaying Dalton's words from earlier today, which made my stomach flip like it never has before.

He's funny, sweet, ridiculously sexy, and even with his choice of eight beautiful, successful celebrities, he wants to go out with *me*. We can't do it, of course, but it feels pretty amazing to know he even wants to.

"Straps up or down?" Farrah asks me.

We're in her bedroom, getting her ready for the sunset cruise. Even though Alex said there's limited space on the boat, especially for someone like me who has to be off camera at all times, Farrah insisted I have to go.

So I'm wearing cutoff jean shorts and a Ramones T-shirt while helping her plan a much classier outfit. It took more than an hour, but she finally agreed to wear a blue dress with ruffled straps that could either be on or off the shoulder.

"Down," I say, setting them into place for her.

"I hate the way the show's makeup artist does my eyes, I want you to do my makeup."

"Uh..." I glance at my phone. "I can, but we'll have to hurry."

"So tell me again what Dalton said about me."

My heart pounds nervously. Dalton and I agreed that we'd let Farrah assume our walk earlier was about him wanting to know more about her. It seemed like a good idea until she hit me up for full details. Now I'm openly lying to her, which I don't feel good about.

"I already told you everything. He's a Midwestern guy. He wants to know about your family and what you're looking for."

"Did you tell him my parents are divorced?"

"I think so."

She balks. "How can you not remember?"

"Sorry."

"Did you tell him I'd have two kids using a surrogate?"

"Yes."

"And? Did he seem okay with it?"

*It'd absolutely be you.*

"Uh, I couldn't tell."

"Alice. For fuck's sake, you're killing me."

A distraction. I need to create a distraction. "Should we use that glowy spray stuff on your shoulders and arms?"

"Oh, good idea. Yes. Did I tell you Dalton held every door for me last night and stopped after just a goodnight kiss? I think he's looking for a wife, Al. He's being such a gentleman."

My skin prickles at the mention of the kiss *again*. Maybe he was just being nice with that compliment earlier. It's easy to tell someone you wish you could go out with them when there's no way you can.

"I never realized how sexy hockey players are. All that fighting. I bet he'd fight any guy who even looked at me the wrong way."

"The glow spray is in my room, I have to go get it."

"Okay, but hurry. And remember to pack tampons. I'm going to need them."

"Already did."

As soon as I get to the hallway, I take a breath and check my phone.

*Will: The home health nurse checked on dad for me. He's good. Went to his therapies today.*

Relief courses through me.

*Alice: Great. Thanks for letting me know.*

Dad is doing okay. That makes it easier to pretend I care about how glowy Farrah's skin looks.

I go to my room and get the spray. I'm making my way back to Farrah's room when I see Dalton coming down the open stairway I'm going up. His gaze darkens just slightly as he looks me over.

"Hey," I say, trying to sound casual even though my pulse is pounding.

"Hey." He leans over to speak next to my ear in a low tone. "You look sexy as hell in those shorts."

His words and the warm brush of his breath against my ear send a jolt of electricity from the tip of my spine to the base. I want to respond, but is "thanks" the right thing to say?

We've already passed each other when he calls out, "You're coming tonight, right?"

*You're coming. You're coming. Oh God, stop it, Alice.*

"Yep, I'll be there!" My voice is an octave too high, but I'm hanging on by a thread here.

I don't look back, rushing to get to the top of the stairs and around the corner. By the time I get to Farrah's bedroom, she's sitting on the edge of the bed, wearing an impatient expression.

"I need a Brazilian."

I close the door. "Um...I can try to get an aesthetician here tomorrow."

"No, for tonight. My vag is still smooth, but I can't see around back well enough to know if it's okay. What if Dalton wants to come back to my room tonight? I can't have a hairy butthole."

*Lord, give me strength.*

"The hair all grows back at the same rate, so if the front's still smooth, so is the back. I have the glow spray."

"Will you look? Just to be sure?"

I gape at her. "At your asshole? No fucking way."

"Come on, Al. You've seen it all anyway."

I laugh, not amused. "I actually haven't seen you bent over spreading your cheeks, and I don't want to. This is a Meatloaf moment."

"For God's sake. Is that the thing where you'd do anything for love, but you won't do that?"

"Exactly." I shake the bottle of spray. "Now let's do this so I can get your makeup done."

❄

THE SUPERYACHT TAKING US ON THE SUNSET cruise is a sailboat, and it's beautiful. Every surface is bright, gleaming white or sparkling silver. Servers are carrying trays of drinks and appetizers, Alex telling them they have five more minutes before they have to stay off camera.

I'm sitting in the small area reserved for the film crew next to the makeup artist, Giana. Misty Meyers is standing with us, all of us chowing on the appetizers Farrah won't even touch.

"Little wieners are underrated," Giana says, holding up a small bacon-wrapped sausage on a stick.

"Depends on how much meat you like," Misty says.

"Meat's good," I muse. "But also, little wieners know how to compensate for their lack of meat, if you know what I mean."

"That part," Giana says. "My boyfriend isn't hung, but that man gives oral like it's his full-time job. He says it's how he keeps his beard so soft and supple. By just burying his face in my snatch."

"Jelly." Misty sighs.

"What, you're not into any of these guys?" I ask.

She shrugs. "There's one guy I like, but he's got his eye on someone else."

"Which one?" Giana asks.

Misty looks at me. "It doesn't matter."

She doesn't want me to know. This means it has to be...

"Dalton?" My heart hammers just from saying his name.

She shakes her head.

"Ah. JP."

"Girl, you're a catch," Giana says. "Don't assume he doesn't like you. Get over there and try."

Misty's smile slides away. "I can't. I'm not..."

Her gaze is on Farrah, who's laughing at something JP just said, her perfect white teeth on display.

"Hold up." I set my plate down, giving her my full attention. "I know I didn't just hear you saying what you're *not*. Because you're here due to what you *are*. Smart. Generous. A silver medalist in the damn Olympics. A world-class athlete. A beautiful, strong woman who inspires girls every day."

She gives me a grateful look. "I know. I'm proud of my accomplishments. But lots of men just want long, lean legs and curves and I'm"--she looks down at her body--"all muscle."

"You're stunning, Misty," Giana assures her. "Ninety-nine plus percent of women could never wear that dress."

I nod. Misty is wearing a formfitting bright-white dress with a halter neck. It's a beautiful contrast to her light-brown skin. Her red-framed sunglasses and strappy red sandals are perfect accents.

"Where the hell is Meyers?" Alex yells. "She did get on the boat, right?"

Misty groans. "That's my cue. Bye, guys."

She goes over to the rest of the cast, and Alex throws his arms in the air when he sees her.

"Can we finally start filming? We're already twenty minutes behind."

I pick up my plate, holding my fork against it so the wind can't pick up either thing and make noise while the cameras are rolling. There are several camera operators on the boat tonight, all of them working at the same time. There's limited light and Alex wants to get as much footage as he can.

"Lorenzo!" Alex says. "Can I trouble you to get your ass over here?"

Dalton, who was talking to a production

assistant, smiles good-naturedly and walks over to the place Alex wants him. He sits down on the other side of Farrah, sandwiching her between the two athletes.

It occurs to me, then, that in setting up a competition for Farrah between Dalton and JP, Alex has pretty much shut Misty out. She gets airtime, but there's no one guy the producers seem to be steering her toward.

Dalton and JP start their usual banter, Farrah radiant as they both focus their attention on her. I feel off when I watch Dalton looking at her, his arm slung casually over the seat behind her.

Probably best not to look at him. Our conversation from our walk earlier is still playing on repeat in my head, and so is that hug. It was so much more than a hug, really. It was the first time in forever that a man had held me. I'm always the one doing the caretaking, never the one receiving the care. It felt good to just let go of everything in his arms, even if it was only for a minute.

We walked for an hour and a half, going all the way to the pier and then past it before we turned around. I told him more about my family, and he told me about the single mom who raised him and his sister, a strong Italian woman. I can't remember the last time anyone listened to me like he did and truly showed interest in what I was saying.

*It'd absolutely be you.*

I force myself to focus on Misty and Dom, who are talking about music. Dom likes a wide variety of music, which I wouldn't have guessed. He got his start playing a drum set that was in the back room of a Laundromat his parents bought. While they worked, he played.

"How about you?" he asks Misty. "What made you start gymnastics?"

"I watched the Olympics on TV and knew I wanted to be there someday. I was the only Black girl in my class and the more the other girls made fun of me, the harder I worked."

Dom holds her gaze, something passing between the two of them.

"That's badass," he says. "And look at you now."

"It took a lot of hard work to get here. It takes even harder work to *stay* here."

"Gotta make some time for fun, too, though. You're too young and beautiful to work all the time."

Giana pokes me and we exchange a look. I sneak a glance at Dalton and our eyes lock.

Holy shit. He is looking at me.

This is starting to feel dangerous. I can't pursue a man Farrah's interested in. Just the thought is laughable.

I look away again, reminding myself what's at stake.

*Everything.*

My dad's care, my parents' home, even my brother's career. If I can't make enough to support our parents, he'll drop out of medical school so he can help me support them.

I can't let that happen. There's too much on the line. A man like Dalton is just a dream for me. Maybe someday I can have that, but not right now.

ten

## DALTON

"What's up with you?" JP asks me over breakfast the next day. "You're normally a lot chattier than this."

I shrug and push the last bite of my omelet around on my plate. "Just tired."

"Did Farrah go back to your room last night? You can tell me if she did."

"No, she didn't."

The sunset cruise sucked. Alice wouldn't even look at me for most of it. I shouldn't have hoped for time alone with her while the entire cast and crew were packed onto a sailboat, but I did.

She looked so damn cute in those jean shorts and that T-shirt. The shorts fit her round ass perfectly and I couldn't stop looking at it.

The female contestants on the show were all made up and wearing dresses, and the guys all had to wear nice pants and collared shirts. But as the sun was setting and the boat was cutting through the waves, I was wishing I could be walking on the beach with Alice, wearing shorts and a T-shirt myself.

Maybe we'd walk to a beachfront restaurant for dinner. Spend hours talking and laughing over a bottle of wine.

It's fucking maddening, falling for a woman so hard and fast and instead having to pretend I want someone else.

I'm over the show. Faking shit isn't for me. But I can't leave. Not only because of Rita and the league but because then I wouldn't get to see Alice anymore. I'll pretend to be interested in *anyone* if it means I can stay here.

Alice wasn't at sunrise yoga this morning. Farrah said she was feeling run down and needed some extra rest. I was disappointed, because even though I couldn't have had a real conversation with her, at least I could've seen her.

"What are you looking for here?" I ask JP. "Are you hoping to find a wife?"

He shrugs. "I wouldn't mind it. I'm thirty, you know? I want to be in a relationship with someone for at least a couple of years before I pop the question, so I know it's right."

"Yeah. But do you worry about having enough time for it? I know football's not as demanding as hockey, but it does take up the occasional weekend."

"Shit." He laughs, then turns serious again. "I know that's part of it, but if you find the right woman, she knows what it takes to play at our level, and she supports it. I can't be with a woman who feels like she's in competition with football for my time. I've been there and done that."

I nod because I've dated women like that, too.

"That's why I'm here, actually," JP says. "All the women here are successful. They have their own careers, and they know what it takes to stay at the top."

"Yeah."

I thought that was important to me, too. But Farrah couldn't be more out of touch with the people and the world around her. I can't be with a woman who is so self-centered.

Alice is *good*. She cares more about taking care

of her family than she does her own happiness. She doesn't want the spotlight. She listens. I find those things about her so attractive that I can hardly think about anything other than her.

"You think Alice is okay?" I say.

JP shrugs. "Yeah, Farrah said she's just tired."

"I'm going to bring her some breakfast."

He rolls his eyes. "Good one. Looking in on the assistant. I should've thought of that."

I meet his gaze, annoyed. "It's got nothing to do with Farrah."

"Sure it doesn't."

I don't care what he thinks. I take my dishes to the kitchen, then ask a kitchen assistant to make a cheese omelet I can drop off for Alice. While they're working on it, I go over to the breakfast buffet and make her a bowl of fresh fruit.

The kitchen assistant gets me a wood tray and a metal dome to cover up the food. I grab bottles of apple juice and water, stuffing one into each pocket.

"How do I get to the staff rooms" I ask. "And do you know which room Alice is in?"

The assistant gives me directions, and I go through a door in the kitchen to reach the hallway that leads to the staff rooms. Alice's is the one at the end of the hall.

I knock on the door softly, not wanting to wake her up if she's asleep. When there's no answer, I knock again.

I could just leave the tray outside the door for her. But I don't want to. I turn the door handle, cracking the door open a couple of inches so I can see inside.

It's a tiny, darkened room with no windows. I can see Alice's dark hair spilling out over the top of the blanket cocoon she's wrapped up in. A fan on the floor is running at high speed, drowning out sound and cooling the stuffy room a little. It doesn't seem like the air conditioning reaches this part of the house.

I walk into the room quietly, wishing I could see her face. But her back is to me and I don't want to disturb her sleep. The bedside table is way too small to hold the tray, so I set it on the floor instead.

I should've put a flower on it. Hopefully the food will be enough to brighten her day.

There are so many things I want to say to her. I want her to know I wanted to be by her side last night, not Farrah's. I want to tell her I've never had such strong feelings for a woman so quickly. That I'm here to listen or hold her. Whatever she needs.

But she works hard, and she needs this rest. So I

tiptoe out and close the door again, going to find Alex for my daily production meeting.

"So what are you looking for?" Farrah asks me that evening, seated beside me in one of the hot tubs. "Just fun or something more?"

Fuck. How do I answer that question? I don't want to say I'm just looking for fun because then she'll think I want to sleep with her. But if I say I want something more, she'll think I want to sleep with her *and* have a relationship with her. I can't win.

Alex told me during our meeting today that it's time to "move past the PG shit and start getting physical." And believe me, I want to. Very badly. Just not with Farrah.

"I don't know," I say in answer to Farrah's question. "It depends, I guess."

"Cut!" Alex yells, launching himself out of his director's chair. "Look, Lorenzo, I get that it's hard for you non-actors to have cameras filming your intimate conversations and all, but you're killing me. Literally ending my fucking existence. I need *chemistry*. Stop looking over at me. Look at her. Put your arm around her. Nibble her ear a little. Make us wonder where your hands are wandering under the water."

I nod because I get where he's coming from. I've seen these reality shows a time or two. Hell, I'm pretty sure Dom and Misty are an actual thing right now because June told everyone she saw Dom doing a walk of shame out of Misty's room this morning.

But it's a lot harder when you're not feeling it. Especially when the woman you are having feelings for is watching the entire thing. It's not Dom I keep looking at, it's Alice.

She won't even look at me. Every time I tried to get her attention today, she avoided me. I get that she doesn't want to piss Farrah off, but it's driving me crazy.

"Follow my lead," Farrah says, putting a hand on my knee.

The cameras start rolling again, and she snuggles closer to me.

"I want to find something real," she says, her tone earnest and sultry at the same time. "Someone who can see me at my worst and still be there."

"Everyone deserves that."

Her hand slides up my leg, her fingernails

grazing my inner thigh. She leans her forehead against my temple, humming with amusement.

"I like that you're a gentleman. But it's okay to be...not a gentleman, too. I like you, Dalton."

I have to suck it up. I'm here to perform, and even though I'm not willing to get any more physical than this, I'm likely to get kicked off the show if I don't show any interest in Farrah.

"I like you, too."

I turn my face just slightly toward hers, waiting for Alex to cut. Farrah puts her free hand on my cheek, easing it over so we're face to face. She puts her lips on mine, kissing me softly and gently.

Though I don't open my mouth, I still kiss her back. One arm stays behind her but not touching her and the other is beside me on the molded seat of the hot tub.

She slides her hand onto my dick, stroking it. "Should we go to my room?"

"Yeah, sure."

A few more agonizing seconds pass, guilt slicing through me as I wonder whether Alice knows Farrah has her hand on my dick.

"And cut," Alex says. "Beautiful, guys."

I stand up as quickly as I can. "Get what you needed?"

"Yes, sir. I would like a shot of you guys walking to the bedroom hand in hand, though. Go ahead and dry off. It doesn't look great when you're dripping water all over the place."

I glance at Alice, who's sitting in her chair, looking at her phone. I hate myself for what I just did.

"No, I think it's implied," I say. "I'm done for tonight."

"Oh, I forgot that you're the director," Alex says dryly.

I grab my towel and dry off my chest and arms. "I'm done. It's nothing personal."

"I agree," Farrah says from the hot tub. "Let's give people room to wonder what came next and assume for themselves. Alice, towel."

Alice springs up to get her towel, avoiding my gaze. She passes by me, just a couple feet away, but I can't say any of the things I want to say.

Farrah gets out of the hot tub and asks Alice to dry her off. It's all I can do not to tell Farrah to fuck off and stop being such an asshole to Alice.

"Let's go for a drive," Farrah says to Alice. "I haven't driven in forever, and we have a convertible."

"Okay."

Alice stays by Farrah's side as they gather their things, Farrah wrapping a long skirt at her waist and fastening it. She flicks a quick gaze to me as they're walking away--it only lasts a second, and I can't discern the emotions swimming in her eyes.

It's nothing good, though, which is exactly what I deserve.

_eleven_

## ALICE

"Hey, wake up. It's seven forty. Are you sick or something?"

I push the covers aside, sitting up and giving Farrah a puzzled look. What's she doing in my room?

"I told you in the text I haven't been sleeping well and I was too tired for sunrise yoga. It's better for you to be alone with Dalton and JP anyway."

She uses the light on her phone to find the way from the doorway to the end of my bed, where she sits down.

"This room is tragic. Why does it smell like fish?"

"Because they store food in here sometimes."

"It's disgusting. There's not even a window."

I shake my head and run a hand over my wild hair, still groggy. "It's fine. I sleep great in here. That's all that matters."

"I'm worried about you, Al. It's the fourth morning in a row you've skipped yoga."

I switch on the bedside lamp, illuminating the room in a dim glow. Then I slide out of bed and get my robe from the hook on the back of the door.

"You have a video conference call with Mateo, Jim and Madison at nine. I bumped your production meeting with Alex to ten twenty in case the conference call runs late. Filming starts at one today. The producers are going to randomly assign one-on-one dates for everyone."

She groans. "That's pointless. I have no chemistry with anyone but Dalton and JP."

All my worries about my parents come rushing back at once. That's what's been keeping me up at night, tossing and turning as I try not to think about my dad suffering. Have I done the right thing, taking care of them financially even though it means I hardly ever get to see them? Will my dad pass away before I get to see him again?

"I have to go to the bathroom," I tell Farrah, glad I have an excuse to escape our endless ongoing conversation about Dalton and JP.

I wouldn't have even considered thinking about Dalton before. He's out of my league, and I'm too overwhelmed by my family situation to seek anything with a man.

But the way he held me on the beach that day...the way my heart leaped when he told me he'd choose me to take on a date...that flip in my stomach when he said I looked sexy in my shorts...

It feels good when he looks at me. At Alice Morrow, the woman, instead of "Farrah's assistant," which is what I am to everyone outside of my family. But it also makes me long for something I can't have.

Watching him and Farrah in the hot tub gutted me. I tried to avoid looking at them, but my eyes kept dragging themselves back. They kissed. And who knows? Maybe he did go up to her room that night. She probably would have told me if he did, but I still can't help wondering.

I've managed to avoid Dalton like a pro. He's a big part of why I've skipped morning yoga, even though I do really need the extra sleep. And when I see him coming my way at the house, I strike up a conversation with whoever is close by.

I'm just too fragile right now for the conversation I know he thinks we need to have. About how he has to show interest in the contestants. How he wishes I could be a contestant on the show, too. His high-pressure job and the demands on him to have a partner who's also famous.

Crying in front of him once--over my family-- was enough. I'm not letting him see me crumble over him not being able to date me. Logically, I get it. Agree with it, even. But I'm also a person, and I get lonely.

I use the bathroom, brushing my teeth with the toothbrush and toothpaste I keep in my robe pocket, and when I get back to my room, Farrah's still sitting on my bed.

"How far is the bathroom?" she asks me.

"It's at the other end of the hallway."

"And you have to shower in there, too? In a bathroom a bunch of other people use?"

"The showers are in the other staff quarters, where the chef's room is."

She wrinkles her nose. "Do you think the maids

here have to clean everything else plus the bathrooms they use? That would suck."

"I'm sure they do. Just like the kitchen staff eats some of the food they cook."

"I'd gag if I had to clean a toilet."

My toiletry bag is stacked on top of a tall pile of Farrah's luggage. I pick it up and say, "Speaking of showers, I need to take one. Did you finish your workout?"

She gets up. "I did a forty-five-minute one since I have that meeting at nine. I guess I should go get ready, too."

"Do you want breakfast before the meeting?"

"I'll take a protein shake and two egg whites."

"Okay, I'll have it ready fifteen minutes before the meeting."

I wait for her to walk out of the room, but she stays beside the bed, crossing her arms and scrunching her face in thought. "What do you think about last night?"

"Last night? You mean the keratin treatment I did on your hair? I think it looks good."

I have an hour to take a shower, dry my hair and get ready, make Farrah's breakfast and hopefully squeeze in a call to my parents. But she's not in any hurry to go.

"No, *Dalton*. The hot tub. Am I making the right choice? JP is taller than him. And a quarterback boyfriend is the ultimate, you know?"

"I think a good person you love being with is the ultimate."

She rolls her eyes. "They both seem like good guys. You know what I'm saying. Pulling JP Covington would get me a lot more visibility."

"You already have tons of visibility on your own."

Why am I making the case for her to *not* choose JP? I'm just being honest because that's my default. But if she ends up with Dalton and I have to scout out the restaurants they go to for dates and take the sheets off her bed after he stays the night with her, that will be really hard.

"I want tall kids, though."

Farrah and I have had some great times together. She's a weird mixture of inconsiderate and generous. But sometimes I want to scream at her. This is one of those times.

"I guess, go with JP then," I say, exasperated.

"Dalton smells better, though. And I can tell he's amazing in bed."

I furrow my brow. "How can you tell that?"

"Just by the way he moves. And his confidence.

And his body, obviously. I pay attention during yoga. He could do me in any position imaginable."

A white-hot bolt of jealousy shoots through me. The thought of them in bed together is too much. I have no right to be this jealous, but I am.

"We need to get moving," I say, swallowing my feelings.

"Okay, you're right."

I open the door, my gaze going straight to the wood tray on the floor. *Shit.* I forgot.

Every day that I've skipped sunrise yoga, Dalton has left me a breakfast tray. Yesterday's had a note from him that said, *Miss seeing you flip off the sky. Feel better soon.*

It made me smile.

"At least they bring you breakfast," Farrah says breezily, stepping around the tray. "Since this room is basically a prison cell, it's the least they can do."

My heart rate slows as she walks down the hallway. I dodged a bullet. If she had asked me who brought the tray, I probably would have panicked.

I take the tray into my room and set it on the bed. There's a red rose in a little vase, a note tucked beneath it. When I peek beneath the silver dome over the plate, I see a decadent cheese omelet, just like the ones he brought the first three days. There's also a bowl of berries and two pieces of bacon.

I'm going to devour this. It's so much better than what I usually get for breakfast here, which is whatever's left after the contestants and crew have ransacked the buffet. I'm too busy making Farrah's food and prepping her waters in the morning to get to breakfast when it's served.

I take out the note, carefully unfolding it.

*We're talking today.*

My stomach does a nervous flip. I want to talk to him, but I also don't. It doesn't sound like I'm going to have a choice, though.

twelve

## DALTON

*DALTON: HOW DID YOU KNOW TRIN WAS THE ONE?*

I'm on a lounger by the pool, waiting for my brother-in-law and best friend, Linc, to text me back. I've got a break from filming this afternoon, so I swam laps to burn off some nervous energy.

Alice is out with Farrah. I'm eager for them to get back because I haven't even seen Alice today. I heard Farrah's voice in her bedroom when I was bringing breakfast this morning, so I just left the tray.

Not seeing her is making me crazy. Even though I can't say what I want to say to her when other people are around--which is always because there are like thirty people in the beach house at any given moment--at least I usually get to see her. Checking her out without getting busted for it is my new pastime.

*Lincoln: You really want to know?*

I cock my head as I read the message, narrowing my eyes at my phone screen.

*Dalton: Spare me the intimate details, and for fuck's sake don't tell me the only way you knew my sister was the one is because of the sex.*

*Lincoln: I knew I loved her before we left the cabin. But when I got back home, that's when I knew. Home didn't feel like home anymore. She did.*

A splashing sound makes me glance up, and I see June getting into the pool. She bites her lip, trying to look seductive, I think? I give my phone my full attention.

*Dalton: I know this sounds crazy. I met someone here and I can't think about anything but her. Haven't even kissed her yet.*

*Lincoln: Why not? Never alone with her?*

*Dalton: The producers and league people have this show scripted. They tell me who to fake chemistry with. It's not what I expected.*

*Lincoln: Really? You thought a reality show would be something other than manufactured drama?*

*Dalton: Good talk, man. Helped a lot.*

I set my phone on the table beside me, put my sunglasses on and lie back in the chair. Just like every time I close my eyes at night, I imagine Alice's face when she pulled away from me on the beach. There was so much vulnerability and gratitude swirling in her eyes.

She's so used to being the listener. The planner. The doer. I want to be those things for her. I want to make her smile and laugh and...other things, too.

What do her eyes look like when she's turned on? How does she sound when she moans? Does she ever completely let go and give in to what she really wants?

And more importantly, could that be me? It would be fucking brutal to finally feel this way about a woman who doesn't feel the same way in return. I've definitely felt something from her, but I don't know if it's just surprise or her indulging me with kindness.

I have to find out. I need to know if this thing is one-sided. That's why I gave her that note this morning.

A kitchen attendant comes out with a tray of

drinks, offering me a lemonade. I drink half of it, dehydrated from the sun, and then check my phone.

*Lincoln: Sorry. I'm happy for you, that you found someone you're into. You think she could be the one?*

*Dalton: I don't know. It feels as crazy as it sounds. But I can't stop thinking about her. I hate having to fake interest in other women here.*

*Lincoln: That sounds dicey. Does she have to fake interest in other guys?*

*Dalton: No, because she's not a contestant.*

*Lincoln: The plot thickens...*

*Dalton: She works for one of the contestants.*

*Lincoln: Are you able to talk to her? Or would it put you in an awkward spot?*

*Dalton: Awkward spot, but doing it anyway.*

*Lincoln: Good for you. Gotta shoot your shot.*

*Dalton: How's the fam?*

*Lincoln: Good. Trin convinced me to take in a litter of 5 puppies someone dumped by the side of the road. So just when Micah starts sleeping through the night, we're bottle feeding puppies.*

*Dalton: You can't say no to dogs, though.*

*Lincoln: Nope. That's how we ended up with eleven of them, plus 5 puppies.*

*Dalton: Good luck with that.*

*Lincoln: Good luck with your thing, too. Lemme know how it goes.*

*Dalton. I will.*

"Come on in, the water's perfect," June purrs.

I glance up from my screen. She's wearing a tiny white bikini, her nipples and areolas visible through the scraps of fabric on top.

"I have to go make a call," I say, getting up.

"You're no fun!"

June and I have different definitions of fun. But I just wave and don't look back. My only concern today is making sure I get some time alone with Alice.

IT'S ALMOST TEN THIRTY THAT NIGHT WHEN ALICE comes walking down the hallway to her room, stopping when she sees me sitting on the floor next to her door, my back against the wall.

"Dalton. What are you doing?"

I nod toward my phone screen. "Watching the last game of the playoffs. I choked so hard it was almost impressive."

She lowers her brows, glancing over her shoulder at the door she just closed behind her, which leads from the kitchen to this staff quarters hallway.

I stand up, my legs tingly from spending the past hour and a half sitting here.

"You know what I meant," she says in a hushed tone, walking toward me.

"I told you we'd be talking today."

She stuck like glue to Farrah today, deliberately not giving me a chance to get her alone. I don't know if she's playing hard to get or if she just doesn't want to talk to me. Either way, it's making me insane.

"I didn't mean any of that in the hot tub with Farrah the other night."

Her eyes widen and she puts a finger over her lips. "Someone might hear."

"You want to talk in your room?"

She considers for a second, then opens the door and steps inside. I follow, and she closes the door behind us.

"Dalton, I--"

"Let me go first. I really like you, Alice." She shushes me again, and I can't help smiling. "I don't care who knows."

"You can't blow Farrah off," she whispers, her eyes pleading with me. "She wants you."

"I don't want her, though."

She closes her eyes, then opens them and sighs heavily. "Look, I know she seems like a lot. But she--"

I eat up the distance between us with two steps, cupping her cheek. "You're not hearing me. I like *you*. I want *you*."

Her lips part as she looks up at me, silent for a moment. "But you don't even know me."

"I know enough to know I want to know a lot more."

"But Farrah--"

I put a finger over her lips, silencing her. "There's only one name I want to hear you say, and it's *mine*. So say it for me."

She inhales sharply, just looking at me. I stroke my thumb over her cheek, putting my other hand on her hip.

"Dalton." She breathes my name, and it lights a fire inside me.

"Do you want me to kiss you as much as I want to kiss you?"

Her single nod is all the encouragement I need. I bend slightly and slant my lips over hers, sliding my hand around to the small of her back. She moans softly, her lips warm against mine.

There's a pounding sledgehammer in place of my heart, my entire body relieved she wants me back and simultaneously so turned on I don't know how I'll stand it. She opens to me, our tongues meeting for the first time.

I deepen the kiss and she puts her arms around my neck, pressing her body against mine.

*Fuck.* I can't take as much as I want. Not tonight. But damn, do I want to. My erection is molded against her stomach, and she seems anything but shy about it. Her fingers rake through my hairline at my neck and she tugs.

I move my hand down, cupping her ass and making her gasp into my mouth. She breathes against my lips for a couple of seconds and then I capture her lips with mine again, not ready for our first kiss to be over.

She matches my passion, both of us breathless when she pulls away. I kiss the line of her jaw and she sighs, her breath warm on my throat.

"I can't stop thinking about you, Alice."

"I...think about you, too."

"I didn't kiss her the other night. She kissed me. I shouldn't have let her, though. I'm sorry."

"It's okay."

"No, it's not. If you can't kiss anyone else, neither can I."

She hums with amusement. "Why can't I kiss anyone else?"

"Because I said so. Unless you don't mind me knocking their teeth out."

She laughs lightly. "Dalton."

"God, I love the sound of you saying my name."

She puts a palm on my chest, leaning back slightly. Regret is etched into her face and reflected in her eyes. "I can't lose my job. If I could--"

"So we'll keep it a secret, then."

"If she finds out--"

"She won't." I take her hand and put her palm over my heart. "I'm having some strong feelings for you, and if you want to see if there's something there for you, too, I'll stay. But if not--if you don't want to give me a shot--then I'm leaving the show. I'll let the producers come up with some bullshit reason for it, but I don't want to be here just to pretend I'm having feelings for someone else."

"No," she whispers. "Don't go."

I lean my forehead against hers, relief washing through me. "I'm here for as long as you want me to be."

Our hands brush, and I lace our fingers together. She smiles, her expression turning shy.

"Get some sleep." I kiss her forehead. "Sunrise yoga starts early."

"Mmm...I think I prefer sleeping in and having a hot guy deliver me breakfast."

I give her a soft, slow kiss. "I prefer getting to look at your ass in yoga pants."

She laughs lightly. "*My* ass? When there's a choice between mine and Farrah's?"

"Hell yes, your ass. It's hot."

"You're sweet."

I shake my head. "I'm not, though. I'm hard as hell, and it's because of *you*. You're the one who does this to me, Alice."

I put her hand over my erection. She inhales sharply and moves her hand, making me groan.

It takes all my willpower to step back. I hold her gaze and say, "See you at sunrise?"

She nods. I open the door and look at her over my shoulder. "I want you to know I'm serious. I'm not just trying to get you in bed."

The corners of her lips curl up slightly. "Okay, Dalton."

I shake my head, forcing myself to turn the handle, open the door and step into the hallway.

The sound of her saying my name is going to be the death of me.

"Good night," I whisper.

"Night."

I close the door, adjusting myself on the walk down the hallway. Our secret won't last an hour if someone sees me walking out of this hallway with a raging boner.

*thirteen*

ALICE

"Isn't it beautiful?" I turn my phone and move it so my parents can see the ocean.

I want to show them the house, too, but photos and videos are strictly prohibited by the contracts everyone had to sign. They've only been to the beach once, though, so my mom is wowed by the view here.

"I'd. Rather. See. You." My dad's computerized voice says, responding to the words he pecks out with his hand.

I put the camera back on my face. "Okay, me again!"

"I can't believe you get to wake up there every day, honey," my mom says, wonder in her tone. "It's like a painting."

After sunrise yoga, Dalton locked his gaze onto mine and gave me a secret wink. It filled me with happiness, and it made me realize something.

Farrah can be ridiculous, but I also let her take advantage of me. I told her to text me after her workout so I could make her breakfast. Instead of spending her workout time taking a five-minute shower and prepping things for her, I took a walk so I could FaceTime my parents.

"I miss you guys," I say as I walk toward the pier.

"We miss you, too," Mom says, wistful. "But we know you're having adventures and making memories, and we're so proud of you."

"Does Dad have therapy today?"

"He has speech therapy at eleven fifteen."

"How's that going, Dad?"

He types out an answer. "Still. Sound. Like. A. Computer. When. I. Speak."

I smile, glad he's still cracking jokes. "I think you should go on the road, Dad. Make a stand-up routine and kill with these jokes every night."

He types, his brow furrowed with concentration. "The. Stand. Up. Part. May. Be. A. Challenge."

"There's your angle. The world's first sit-down comic."

There's a ringing sound in the background and my mom cringes slightly. "That's the home nurse, honey. We have to go."

"Okay, bye guys!" I wave at them and blow a kiss. "I love you."

"Love you, too," Mom says.

I wait for Dad to finish typing out a message to me. "Keep. Shining."

I blow him another kiss and end the call, tears flooding my eyes. He's been saying that to me since I was a kid and it warms me like I just got a hug from him.

As I head back toward the beach house, I feel lighter. This was exactly what I needed. Now I'm ready to really start my day. It's not a crazy busy day, but now I have a new challenge: pretending I'm not replaying that kiss on repeat and thinking about Dalton.

THAT EVENING, I'M STILL IN A DAZE AS I PARK THE Bronco and walk to the beach house. The day took a very unexpected turn when Alex switched up the filming schedule. Farrah had an appointment at a local spa for a massage, facial and pedicure, but instead, she and the other contestants were sent on a scavenger hunt as a competition for the show.

It would be an understatement to say she was unhappy. But she did it, and she told me to take her appointments at the salon.

I felt guilty as I was being treated like an A-lister at a posh salon, getting polished and buffed and pampered. If she knew about that kiss last night...

She doesn't, though. I moved past the guilt at the start of the hot stone massage, which was basically heaven on earth.

"Girl..." Misty's eyes widen when I walk into the sunny, plant-filled great room.

"How was it? I haven't heard from Farrah and I'm getting worried."

"She came in next to last in the scavenger hunt. I heard she got mobbed for autographs at a shopping center."

"Oh, crap."

She wanted me to go with her, but Alex told her no way. The other contestants didn't have assistants helping them, so she couldn't, either. That's how I ended up at the spa.

Misty looks over both shoulders to make sure no one is nearby, and then she breaks out into a huge grin. "I have a date with Dom tonight!"

"Good! So you've changed your mind about him?"

Her gaze turns dreamy. "Yeah, I have. He's actually...soulful. He plays his guitar and sings for me, and he's a literal rock star in bed."

"I'm happy for you."

She whispers the next part. "Farrah has a date with Josh Sellers."

My jaw drops. Farrah will be on the warpath for sure. The rising star politician isn't someone she has any interest in a date with. "Oh, God. I better go find her."

"Good luck."

Steeling myself, I go to Farrah's room, where I find her sprawled out starfish style on the bed. She turns her head in my direction as I come into the room and close the door.

"Worst fucking day ever. EVER." She covers her face with her hands and groans. "I didn't even have time to text you because they had me racing all over the place looking for the stupidest shit imaginable. I was so sweaty. And now I have to go on a date with *Josh*."

She sits up, glowering. "How was the spa?"

I hesitate. "Oh, you know. It sucked. There was a power outage and I had an allergic reaction to the facial."

Her brows hike up. "Really?"

"No."

A laugh bubbles out of her. "You always know how to make me laugh. I wish you could've been there with me. I would've come in last place on purpose. It's not like I care about winning a scavenger hunt. Dalton and JP competed like it was the Olympics."

Dalton. My stomach flips just from the mention of his name. "Did one of them win?"

"No, Josh did. Dalton was doing great, but then, apparently, he couldn't find a place that sold strawberry ice cream. How easy is that? There's an ice cream place on every block. So he doesn't get a date tonight."

I keep my expression neutral, not letting my relief show.

"I shouldn't even shower before this date," she says. "I should just make him inhale my funk all night long."

"That's one approach."

She sighs dramatically. "I'd have to smell myself all night long, though. I'll shower, but I'm not wearing perfume and I want you to find me something super unflattering from the wardrobe department."

"Um, a bedsheet is flattering on you."

"True. But you know what I'm saying. Find something that doesn't show any cleavage. We're going mini golfing."

I fight a smile. She's going to hate that.

"Don't you dare laugh." She scowls. "I can't believe I agreed to do this stupid show. Touching a sweaty golf club someone else just used when we could be on a yacht in France."

"I'll make sure the production people have a new golf club for you."

"Fine. I'm taking a shower."

I close the door to her room, waiting until I'm halfway down the hallway to laugh. She'll have to pretend she's having fun for hours, which won't be hard for an actor. And I get the evening off.

Which I deserve. And I'm going to enjoy it.

Dinner at the house that night is a taco bar. I load up two soft shells with meat, cheese and toppings, adding chips with queso and salsa on the side. I'm sitting on one of the patios with dinner, a glass of wine and a book when a deep voice says, "May I join you?"

It's Dalton, and there's a gleam in his eye. I nod, excited and anxious at the same time.

He leaves an empty seat between us, setting down a plate overflowing with tacos and a glass of iced tea.

"Sweet or unsweet?" I ask him.

"You mean me or the tea?"

A smile tugs on my lips. "The tea."

"Unsweet."

"What is it with you and sweets? I hear you had trouble finding ice cream today."

He shrugs. "I choked. Could've been out on a one-on-one tonight, but I had no idea where to look for strawberry ice cream."

My heart leaps. His tone confirms what I already suspected; he deliberately lost today so he could be here. No matter how much I tell myself to stop playing this dangerous game with him, I can't.

It feels too good. It's been so long since I did something just for me. Years. And even then, it was never anything like this. Being with Dalton is heady and indulgent. There's a buzz between us that makes my skin heat and my heart pound.

Some of the other contestants are swimming, yelling as they splash water on each other and line up bottles and cups to make a swim-up bar.

"You feel like taking a walk?" Dalton asks me.

I look away. "Yeah, but I don't think we should."

"Yeah, guess not." He stands up, and I get a sinking sensation when I realize he's leaving.

"I need to return an email from my agent and I have to do it from my laptop because of security." He glances over his shoulder, making sure no one is close enough to hear him. "So if I happen to come by your room around eight, will you be there?"

I should say no, but I don't even consider it. Instead I just nod, not trusting my voice.

His gaze darkens slightly, raking over me like a long, sensual stroke. He picks up his plate and glass from the table, then comes over and takes mine, too.

"See you soon," he murmurs, his lips hardly moving.

I'm so worried about giving away my excitement that I force my mind onto something bland. My grandma used to knit hats. I make a mental inventory of every hat she knitted for me and Will. My favorite one was pink and purple with a giant fuzzy ball on top. He didn't have a favorite; he pretended to love the hats in front of her and then pulled them off and stuffed them into his pockets before anyone at school could see them.

Okay, that helped. I sigh heavily, feigning boredom, and scroll on my phone. Inside, I'm doing jumping jacks, though.

I got all of Farrah's spa treatments today. I'm fully polished, waxed and moisturized. Even if Dalton just wants to hang out and talk, I at least smell nice.

My heart is galloping at full speed, though, because I'm hoping he wants more than that.

I know I do.

_fourteen_

## DALTON

MY MIND WAS NOT ON THAT EMAIL TO MY AGENT. I had to read what he wrote three times just to make sure I knew what he was saying before I responded.

It was an endorsement deal offer for deodorant. I told him to negotiate the best terms and I'll do it if he thinks I should. Why not? Endorsing not smelling bad is a safe bet.

Speaking of...I sniff my pits one more time as I pretend to sit casually in the great room, looking at my phone. There are two entrances to the staff hallway Alice's room is in--one through the kitchen and one from the outside of the house.

I can't risk the outside one because I don't know what the security setup is here. If an alarm sounds, I'd be busted. So I have to wait until there's no one in the kitchen so I can slip through that door.

It's hell, knowing she's so close and pretending I'd rather be sitting here. Every time I looked at her today, I wanted her back in my arms. Our kiss last night is all I can think about.

"Dalton, come out and swim!" June walks out of the kitchen carrying a bottle of wine, wearing a white bikini and a sheer cover-up.

She sounds tipsy. I flick an annoyed glance at her. "No, I'm good."

My anger flares as she walks over to me. I'm not in the mood for her whining. "Come on, Dalty. Have some fun for once."

"I want to be alone."

She huffs out a breath, cradling the bottle close to her chest as she goes over to the doors that lead outside. "Fuck you very much. You don't even get the point of this show."

I don't react. Once she leaves, I wait for her to get several yards from the door before I shoot up from my seat and race into the kitchen. Fucking finally.

Once I'm on the other side of the door, I

breathe a quick sigh of relief and hurry to the end of the hall, where I knock lightly on Alice's door.

She opens the door, motioning me inside. I step in and she closes the door. I take in her casual, formfitting black tank top and red boxers with white hearts, the white straps of her bra peeking out from under the tank top. Her hair is loose and curly around her shoulders.

"You're beautiful," I say, my gaze sliding down her body and then back up again.

We stand that way for a few seconds, me drinking her in with my eyes, my hands flexing at my sides, as she gives me a shy smile. When her eyes slide down to my crotch and she sees my arousal, her smile turns bolder.

"If you wanted to kiss me some more, that might be nice," she says softly.

"Might?" I quirk a brow, amused.

She shrugs, her expression playful. "I can let you know after."

We lunge for each other, my arms encircling her lower back and pulling her body against mine. I kiss her, the longing I've been feeling since I left this room last night coming through in my groan.

She tugs my T-shirt up as she kisses me, moaning as she puts her palm on the bare skin of my back. Her fingers glide up as she explores, feeling my upper back and shoulder.

I squeeze her ass gently, making her inhale sharply. She takes a step back, her gaze locked on mine as she pulls her tank top up and off over her head.

My exhale is long and ragged. Her chest rises and falls as she breathes, her eyes swimming with desire.

"We won't get much time together," she says, and I'm not sure if she means tonight or ever. "So let's not waste what we have."

She reaches around to her back and unfastens her bra, the satin cups gently dropping away from her round, full breasts as she takes it off.

"Fuck," I whisper, awed by her body. "You're sure?"

She nods, an uncertain flicker passing over her face. "Are you?"

"Completely. And if you change your mind--at any point--I won't be disappointed, okay? I want this to be exactly what you want."

A smile plays on her lips as she slowly slides her boxers down, my mouth going dry.

She's perfect. Her body is soft and curvy, her pussy bare and smooth. I could look at her for hours, letting my hunger and appreciation for her build. But she doesn't want to waste time, and I'm too mesmerized to give her anything other than exactly what she wants.

I pull my shirt off over my head and drop it to the ground. Her eyes widen slightly as she looks at my chest and abs, her gaze lingering as I push my shorts and underwear off.

When I cover the few steps between us, she looks up at me, her expression shy. Her nipples are pebbled with arousal, though, and it's hot as hell.

She puts her palm on my chest, sliding it over and then down, exploring the lines and ridges of my body. This time, she goes lower, gently stroking my erection and making me hiss in a breath.

I cup her face in my hands and kiss her, soft and slow. Her touch makes me groan. I've been touched before, of course, but never like this, never by Alice, who knocked me off my feet with a single conversation.

Since that day on the beach, I haven't looked at or thought of another woman. There's just Alice--strong, beautiful, compassionate, vibrant Alice.

She backs against the edge of the room's small bed, sitting on it and then lying back. I gaze reverently at her body, lit by the dim glow of a bedside lamp.

It's different with her. I'm not horny for a night of fun. Instead, I feel a deep, aching desire to please her. I honed my body to perfection, thinking it was for hockey, but it was actually for this. So I could show this incredible woman how sexy she is. So I can give her everything she wants and turn those desires into needs that only I can satisfy.

I get on the bed, balancing my weight on my hands and knees as I kiss her jawline, her neck and her chest. She smoothes her hands down my back, squeezing my ass.

At the same moment, I lick one of her nipples and suck it between my lips, making us both groan. Her back is already arching off the bed. She's fucking starved for this--for me--and I'm going to satisfy her in every possible way.

She whispers my name as I tease her nipples, sliding a hand from her waist down her outer thigh and then hooking it behind her knee.

When my mouth moves lower to her stomach, her breathing turns ragged. She rakes her fingers through my hair and tugs, the sensation making my cock ache with want.

Her pussy is already gleaming with arousal

when I gently run my tongue over her seam, making her gasp. I take my time, kissing softly and teasing with my tongue for a few minutes before sliding my tongue inside her.

I hear her clap her hand over her mouth to stifle her cry. I have the back of her thigh on one of my shoulders, and I slide my other hand up to cup her breast and gently squeeze her nipple as I flick my tongue over her clit.

God, she's incredible. The head of my cock is soaked with precum just from tasting her. When she circles her hips, creating friction between my mouth and her clit, I have to force myself not to get too turned on.

I slide a finger inside her slick folds, her hold on my hair tightening as she pulls. When I add another finger and suck her clit into my mouth, she comes undone, arching up from the bed and breathing hard.

I make sure I've wrung everything I can out of her, not moving my mouth from her until she drops back down to the bed limply.

"I want you inside me," she whispers softly.

"We can wait until you're--"

"No. Now."

I'm not arguing with that; my cock is painfully

hard. I brace myself with a knee beside her thigh and run a hand up and down my shaft, positioning the head at her slick entrance.

It's heaven, sliding the head of my cock inside her. I stop, giving her time to adjust, and she puts a hand on my waist, encouraging me to go in farther.

I exhale hard, her soaked pussy so tight I have to stop. She feels so goddamned good.

"Don't stop," she pleads.

"Babe, I have to. Just for a second."

She puts a hand on my shoulder, pushing me down so she can whisper in my ear.

"You made my pussy this wet. I want you to enjoy it. I can't come again yet, so I want you to do it exactly like you like. Come inside me, Dalton."

Holy *shit*. My entire body trembles with arousal. She's incredible in every possible way *and* she talks dirty in bed? I'm not going to survive this woman.

I slowly sink all the way inside her. A cringe flickers over her face and I stop, pulling almost all the way out.

"No, don't stop. It's just been a long time, but you feel so good. Give it to me. Please."

I could get so fucking hooked on the sound of her saying *give it to me*. I don't know how I got so lucky to get to be her first in a long time, but I'm going to show her how real men take care of a woman in bed.

I get to my knees, grabbing a pillow to slide beneath her bottom. Then I slide a thumb into my mouth, wetting it, and put the soles of her feet on my chest near my shoulders. When I pump my cock all the way into her again, she lets out a broken, satisfied exhale.

I fuck her slowly, sinking all the way in and back out with every stroke. From this angle, I can see everything--her pink, parted lips as she breathes heavily, her breasts shaking with every thrust, her wet pussy taking my entire cock.

As soon as she starts rolling her hips, silently asking me to go faster, I put my thumb in my mouth again, soaking it and circling it over her clit.

She sucks in a sharp breath, holding it.

"Breathe, baby," I whisper. "I'm gonna come in your sweet pussy and you're gonna come again, too."

Her eyes lock with mine, arousal pooling in them as I gently stroke her clit and speed up my thrusts.

"Oh, God," she whispers. "Dalton..."

My body tightens, clinging to the edge of release. I won't go until she does. She's so close.

A few more seconds and her thighs lock up, pressing on my shoulders as she trembles with the force of her orgasm, a hand clamped over her mouth. It only takes a couple more thrusts for me to follow, silently groaning as I spill myself into her.

It's like nothing I've ever felt before. It was my first time coming inside a woman. We should have talked about protection before, but I get tested regularly and I haven't had sex since my last test, so I know I'm good.

That conversation can wait. For now, I just want to live in this moment. I look around the room.

"Do you want some tissues?"

She smiles lazily. "Not yet. I'll get something in a minute."

I stretch out beside her on my side, kissing her forehead, her cheek, her nose, her chin, and then her lips.

"You probably hear this a lot, but that was the most incredible sex of my life," I whisper against her lips.

She laughs softly. "Same, and I'm guessing you're the one who hears it a lot."

I run my hand from her hip to her stomach. "No, Alice. Really. I've never come inside a woman before."

Her eyes widen. "Did I make you do something you didn't want to do?"

"Fuck no. I don't mean it like that. I wanted that more than I wanted to keep breathing, and I'm hoping to do it again later. I just..." I run my fingertips over her jawline. "It's because it's you. I needed this with you."

Her expression softens. "Me too. And I'm on birth control."

I gently trace the lines of her collarbone, her breasts, her shoulder.

"I've never been able to come twice like that," she whispers. "And the second one...I've never come that hard before."

Pride fills my chest. I couldn't be her first, but I'd rather be her best. I trail my fingertips down her body, running them over her smooth, slick slit.

"It's so fucking hot that you're full of my cum right now." I smile sheepishly. "I don't mean to blow off the sweet talk, but your body...I'm hard again already. I want more of you. As much as you'll give me."

I'm already thinking about rubbing a load of cum around the rim of her ass while I eat her pussy. I want to make her come again and again and again.

It was feelings that brought me to her bed, but there's also a raw, animalistic attraction that I can't fight. I want to be with her. In bed. Over breakfast. Out with friends.

I can't tell her that yet, though. She'll think I'm crazy for already being so sure about us.

I am, though. Alice Morrow is the woman I'll never get over if she slips through my fingers.

ALICE

"Good morning."

I greet Farrah with a smile even though it's zero dark thirty and I'm exhausted. Dalton spent his fourth night in a row in my room last night, and even though I made him promise we'd be sleeping by midnight, we were up until almost two a.m.

I'm grateful I do yoga--for the first time ever--because I'd be too sore to walk without it. Between riding him repeatedly, having my knees pushed up to my ears while he pounds me and being bent over more times than I can count, I'm still upright, and that's a win.

"I was hoping you'd get here first," Farrah says, her eyes narrowed. "I'm so fucking pissed, Alice. I don't even want to do yoga today."

Oh, hell yes. Maybe I can go back to bed for a couple of hours.

"What's wrong?"

"Dalton's a snake. That's what's wrong."

My heart skips a beat. She knows. She's going to fire me and I won't be able to help my parents anymore. What was I thinking, being so selfish? I should have known better.

I'm about to spill my guts when she cuts me off.

"He's sleeping with someone in the house, and we're going to figure out who it is."

"Um...what?" My stomach dips like I just tipped over the top of a huge hill on a rollercoaster.

"I knew something was up. He's been so weird with me lately. I went to his room last night at eleven forty-five and he wasn't there."

"Oh."

She doesn't know it's me. This is bad, though, because she'll figure it out. How can I make her second-guess her theory?

"Maybe he was just walking on the beach or something. Or hanging out with JP."

She shakes her head. "I checked everywhere

and I couldn't find him. And I went to check his room again on my way here, at"--she looks at her watch--"five forty-five a.m., and he still wasn't there. His bed is still made."

An alarm blares in my head. It's pretty much just the word *fuck*, stretched out to last about ten seconds. How could we have been so careless? Dalton snuck out of my room around four a.m. after our first two nights together, but he asked if he could stay the night after the third, and it was too tempting to resist.

We thought as long as we arrived separately to sunrise yoga, we'd be okay.

"Mornin', ladies." Dalton strolls up with a lazy grin, and now that I'm paying attention, I can see what Farrah will see.

Under-eye circles. Bed head. The same shorts he wore yesterday. He might as well be wearing a shirt that says, "I just spent the night fucking."

Ugh. I'm going to have to become a stripper to make the kind of money I make working for Farrah, and I don't have the body or the mental fortitude for it.

"Good morning," Farrah says, pasting on a fake smile. "How was your night last night?"

He shrugs. "Pretty quiet. Went to bed early. How was your date with Josh?"

"It was fine."

She starts the yoga session, and I try to seem fresh and well-rested by doing every movement as well as I can and not complaining. It's not the end of the world that she knows Dalton wants someone other than her; it'll just be the end of the world if she finds out it's *me*.

"Sorry, I overslept," JP says as he walks up to us about twenty minutes later.

"That's okay," Farrah says lightly. "At least you're honest. There's nothing worse than a backstabbing liar."

JP wrinkles his brow. "Yeah, I slept through my alarm."

"Return to downward dog," Farrah says.

I don't dare even make eye contact with Dalton. My stomach is churning nervously because I feel like Farrah will see right through me no matter what I do.

"Did Josh keep you out late last night?" JP asks.

"No, not at all. I went to bed early last night, just like Dalton."

She says his name pointedly, making me cringe

inwardly. Maybe I should tell her the truth when she and I are alone.

No, I can't. She'll lose her shit. Say I stole him from her.

Can wheelchairs get repossessed? I imagine a couple of big, scary-looking guys lifting my poor father out of his specialized chair, setting him on the couch and leaving with the chair I haven't quite paid off yet.

Fuck. This is awful. Why did I think this was worth risking my dad's care?

"I feel sick," I say weakly.

I'm desperate to end this yoga session, but I'm not lying. I could throw up any second now.

"Lie down, see if that helps," Dalton says, approaching me.

I curl into myself in the sand, his hand on my shoulder like an electrical jolt.

She'll see. She'll figure it out. Why is he touching me?

"Let's just call it," Farrah says. "I'll stay here with Alice until she feels better."

"Yes!" I muster all the enthusiasm I can. "You guys go do your thing. Farrah will stay with me."

"You want to see how much faster football players can run than hockey players?" JP asks

Dalton. "I'll slow myself down so I don't embarrass you too badly."

Dalton's laugh is halfhearted.

"You sure you're okay?" he asks me.

I want to scream at him to leave. I need time to think before Farrah finds out what we've been up to behind her back.

There's enough money in my bank account to pay off the chair. Will is getting paid now that he's a resident instead of a med student. With my experience, maybe I could get a job as an assistant for another celebrity, even if they don't pay me as much as Farrah does.

"I'm fine," I assure Dalton. "Go run. I just need to rest for a few minutes."

He and JP take off down the beach, my heart returning to a normal rhythm once they're gone. Farrah plops down in the sand next to me.

"God, I hope you don't have the flu or something."

"Yeah, me too."

"I wish you'd listen to me about eating that shitty fast food. If the food doesn't make you sick, the germs from the people's hands making it will."

"Uh-huh." I press my cheek to the cool sand.

"So anyway, we need to work together to figure out who Dalton's fucking. My money's on June."

"You're probably right."

"She made it pretty damn easy for him. She spreads her legs when he walks past."

I laugh lightly because Farrah is a total hypocrite, but she's *my* hypocrite. Despite her many flaws, I like being around her. I just wish I wasn't around her sixteen hours a day, seven days a week.

"Why don't you just go for JP? Like you said, he's taller, and you want tall kids."

She sighs heavily. "I probably will. But I still want to know who Dalton's sticking it in. I can drop a bomb on him during filming if I want."

My nausea returns as I imagine my parents watching *Celebrity Love Malibu* and finding out a contestant has been *sticking it in* their daughter.

"Are you okay to go back to the house?" Farrah asks.

I press myself up to a sitting position with my hand. "Yeah, I think so."

"We'll walk slowly." She stands and brushes the sand from her clothes. "Also, you'll need to wear gloves and a mask when you make my breakfast."

THE SPARK BETWEEN MISTY AND DOM HAS TAKEN Alex's attention, which is an unexpected windfall. The camera operators have been taking shifts waiting outside both Misty and Dom's rooms, catching them leaving after their interludes.

And from what I'm hearing, it's not just in the mornings. Those two also like to have a go at it during the day if they can get away with it.

Good for Misty. She deserves to have a man completely wrapped up in her.

If I could get her alone, I might talk to her about my dilemma. I sense I can trust her. There's not a chance, though. Dom is always there, his arm slung around her possessively.

"Hey, can I help out with that?" I ask one of the kitchen assistants. "I'm not busy."

She looks up, her brows arched with surprise. "You want to take the lunch orders?"

I nod, desperate for an excuse to talk to Dalton. "Yep, no problem at all. Just the rest of the people on that list?"

She passes me the notepad and pen. "Yeah, that'd be great. Bring it to me in the kitchen once you've gotten everyone."

"You got it."

I track down everyone other than Dalton first,

getting their sandwich and side orders. My nausea is much better, but it's still a low-grade, constant presence.

If Farrah confronts me in front of other people, what will I say? Will I defend myself or burst into anxious tears? What if she does it on camera? And worst of all, what if it makes it onto the show?

The word *fuck* plays on repeat in the back of my mind, my soundtrack for today. I imagine it being the main word in popular tunes like "Row, Row, Row Your Boat" and "Happy Birthday."

*Fuck fuck fuck fuck to you...fuck fuck fuck fuck to you....*

"Dalton!" I find him on one of the patios talking to Ben, one of the production assistants. "Do you have a minute for me to get your lunch order?"

"Yeah, of course." He nods at Ben. "I'll catch you later, man."

"Hey, so I just need to find out what you want for lunch." I hold the pen over the pad like I'm about to write it down as we walk.

Once we're alone at the far end of the patio, he says, "Do you know how hard it is not to kiss you right now?"

I keep my expression placid. "Farrah checked

your room last night and this morning. She knows you're sleeping with someone."

"Damn, psycho much?"

"We can't do this anymore."

His expression snaps from carefree to serious. "What? No. She doesn't know it's you."

"Yeah, and she wants me to help her spy on you so she can figure it out. Should I tell her I have a conflict from ten p.m. to four a.m.?"

He shakes his head, a smile playing on his lips. I write "ham and Swiss on wheat" on the notepad, so it looks like I'm doing what I'm supposed to.

"Babe, this isn't a big deal. We'll figure it out. You haven't had a good night of sleep in a while, so everything feels more magnified than it is."

He doesn't get it. He doesn't have anything on the line here, and I have *everything* on the line.

"Don't come to my room tonight."

"You're serious."

"Yes!" I write "fruit" on the notepad. "You know I can't lose my job."

"Hey..." His expression softens. "I've got you. If you need money--"

"No."

He doesn't get it. I can't risk my dad losing his therapies. My mom losing her housecleaning and caregiving help. The word of a man I've been secretly sleeping with for less than a week isn't enough to make me risk those things.

"Please respect what I'm asking." I give him a final pleading look before walking away.

*sixteen*

## DALTON

The screaming and laughing from the contestants in the pool is grating on my nerves. June could announce she's taking her top off without belting it out to everyone within a mile radius.

Things are heating up on the show; people are hooking up. I'm relieved because the heat's off me now. JP is going full throttle after Farrah, and I hope he gets what he wants.

I just don't get why Alice and I can't also get what we want. Instead of spending the evening in bed with her, I'm staring at the rotation of the ceiling fan in my bedroom, fighting my urge to go to her room.

Farrah has put her in an impossible position, and I'm seeing red over it. Because Farrah is demanding, controlling, and out for herself only, Alice is afraid to be with me.

And why? There's zero chance I'm going to be with Farrah now that Alice doesn't want me. I'd leave the show, but then I couldn't even see Alice.

I'm looking at new photos of Micah and watching videos Trin sent me of him, feeling like a caged beast, when Alice finally texts me back.

*Alice: I can't risk her finding out. You know my reasons. If it was just about what I want, you and I would be in my room right now.*

I groan, my cock stirring as I think about burying my face between her thighs.

*Dalton: Where are you?*

*Alice: Sitting on the patio with Farrah. She's keeping track of all the contestants so she can figure out whose room you go into later.*

I slam my phone onto the bed, so pissed off it's all I can do not to go down there and tell Farrah to stay the fuck out of my life. Then I pick it back up and text Alice back.

*Dalton: Someone needs to tell her she's a grown ass*

*adult, not a teenager. Are you saying we're over, just because of her?*

*Alice: I can't do this now, or I'll cry in front of her. I'll text later when I'm in my room.*

I scrub a hand down my face. She's worried about crying because she plans to break things off with me. How can I fix this?

I pace a *U* shape around the bed in my room, thinking. I'm not worked up about tonight in particular; it's knowing Alice thinks we can *never* be together that's the problem.

Maybe I should bide my time. Wait for the show to be done filming and hold off on pursuing a relationship until then.

Will she be willing then, though? Farrah doesn't give her time off, so how could we ever spend time alone?

I sit on the edge of the bed, burying my head in my hands. I've finally met the woman of my dreams, but she's going to have to choose between me and her job. It's not right for me to ask that of her.

Alice is so strong. She's been putting her own wants and needs aside to care for her family for a long time. I shouldn't have asked her to jeopardize that just because I feel so strongly about her.

It hurts--there's an actual, physical ache in my gut--as I realize maybe she'll only ever want to be my friend. As much as I hate seeing her wait on Farrah every day, that's how she makes the money her family needs. I'm not telling her she could do better, because she's doing what she has to in order to take care of her parents. I admire that.

Alice would scrub toilets if that's what it took to make her parents' lives easier. That tenacity and devotion are a big reason why I'm crazy about her.

Loud music is playing outside now, and it almost drowns out the shouting. I can't take knowing Alice is so close--right there on the patio--while I'm here, and I can't go to her.

I grab a baseball hat, put it on, and open the Uber app on my phone. I need a break from this insanity, and I know exactly where I want to go.

seventeen

## ALICE

My pillowcase smells like Dalton. I close my eyes and breathe in the scent, imagining he's here.

When we're snuggling post-sex, I snuggle into his side and wrap my leg around him. He runs his fingertips over my bare skin, spelling out letters to make words on my back.

I can never figure out the letters, and we always end up laughing. If I don't guess it right, he does it again, so it takes a long time for me to finally figure out the words, and they're always random.

Indict. Bacon. Anachronism.

I smile at the memory of our most recent

173

night together in this bed, when he spelled *cat* after I got low-key aggravated over *anachronism*. It's sweet, really, because I told him I've always loved reading and words, and I think he tries to show me with some of the words that he's more than the dumb jock perception a lot of people have of athletes.

He doesn't need to do that, though. I already know much of who he is from our late-night whispered conversations. As the only male in the house for most of his childhood, he felt responsible for his mom and sister. He loves the outdoors and feels guilty about traveling by private plane with his team because of the pollution. If he didn't play hockey, he'd make his living as a ranger in a national park.

I throw the covers aside and get out of bed, my one-minute post-alarm snooze session over. The only upside of being alone last night is that I got a decent night's sleep. Not even my anxiety over Farrah finding out about Dalton could keep me up. After four nights in a row of minimal sleep, I crashed for seven hours.

After putting on my robe, I get my bathroom caddy and go to the bathroom. Every morning I came here after a night with Dalton, I'd grin at myself in the mirror, blissed out and a little stunned that this was happening to me and not Farrah.

Every second was incredible, and I'll never forget it. But it can't continue. I have to put my parents first.

I take a deep breath and look at my reflection in the mirror, my hands braced on the sink in front of me. It won't be easy to see Dalton at sunrise yoga in a few minutes. In fact, every time I see him for the remainder of the filming will be hard.

But it's better than how hard it would be to tell my parents I can't pay for Dad's extra therapies anymore. Better than them worrying about losing their home.

It's a *choose your hard situation*, and I won't be able to live with myself if I don't make the right choice.

I dress in black shorts and a plain gray T-shirt, then slide on my sandals, grab my phone and head toward the kitchen. When I walk through the door that leads from the staff hallway to the kitchen, I see Dalton.

He's leaning against the counter, a stainless water bottle raised to his mouth. His expression changes when he sees me, his intense gaze brushing over me like a soft caress.

"Morning," he says softly.

"Good morning."

My heart races as I walk over to one of the wide stainless refrigerators and take out two glass bottles of water. Just water for me and lavender lemon for Farrah.

I glance over at Dalton, my stomach flipping over the way he's looking at me. A mix of hunger and uncertainty swirls in his eyes. I want to run to him, throw myself in his arms and press every inch of my body against his solid warmth.

We just look at each other for a few seconds, neither of us speaking. The spell is broken when my phone buzzes with an incoming text.

Farrah's probably wondering where I'm at. I pick up my phone and read the message, my heart pounding harder with each word.

*Mom: Dad and I are going to the hospital in an ambulance. The paramedics said he may have had another stroke or a seizure. I'll text as soon as I know something. Love you.*

"No," I whisper, tears filling my eyes.

This is the cost of making enough money to help my parents. My dad, whose condition is already fragile, is on his way to the hospital, and I'm at a beach house in Malibu, completely helpless.

"What is it?" Dalton strides over to me and takes my hand.

"My dad." I blink and the clouds clear from my vision as tears drop onto my cheeks. "My mom called an ambulance. They think he had another stroke or a seizure."

"Babe." His voice is soft and he gently squeezes my hand. "What can I do for you?"

My lips part and I shake my head, at a loss for words. But then, clarity comes.

"I'm going there. I need to be with my dad."

He nods. "You want me to tell Farrah?"

My exhale is heavy. She's not going to take this well. But I don't care. I'm not asking her permission.

"I'll do it, but thanks."

"Want me to go throw some stuff in a bag for you?"

"It's okay. I'm just going to take my bag and my phone. God, I hope I can get a flight there today."

"You will." He gives my hand a reassuring squeeze.

"Okay." I take a steadying breath. "Let's get this over."

Dalton follows me to the usual yoga spot on the beach. As usual, Farrah is the first one there.

"It's cold this morning," she says in greeting. "Will you go grab me a hoodie?"

"I have to go." I blurt it out, my stomach churning with worry.

"Go where?" She pinches her brows together, confused.

"Home. To Michigan. My dad is on the way to the hospital in an ambulance."

Her expression morphs from confused to dismissive. "It'll take you all day to get there. And you won't be able to have your phone on in the air. You can call and check in on him from here."

"No, I'm going."

She scoffs. "I get that it's upsetting, but is he dying or something? It might be nothing."

I've never told Farrah about my family. Mostly because she's never asked, but also because she had a sad childhood. Her father died when she was three and the man her mom remarried was an abusive alcoholic. Despite Farrah breezily telling everyone that she loves going back to Pella, Iowa, for the tulip festival, she never goes home. She hates her mother for what she was put through, and even without knowing the specifics, I understand why.

"Your schedule is on my laptop. Same password I use for everything."

"Alice--"

Emotion clogs my throat. "I'm going. I'm not standing here and arguing about it until you understand. It's not about you."

She's taken aback. I've never pushed back-- on anything.

Dalton clears his throat, looking at his phone screen. "I know a few people in LA. I'll see what I can come up with for a chartered flight."

"Why would you do that?" Farrah snaps. "*I'll* do it."

I press my lips together firmly, shooting Dalton a quick, grateful look. Farrah is highly connected in LA. She knows directors, producers, actors and athletes. But she wouldn't have offered to help me if Dalton hadn't, and as badly as I want to get home, I would never ask.

"I'll have something set up for you when you get to LAX," Farrah says absently. "Where are you flying?"

I've been her assistant for more than three years, and she still doesn't know my hometown.

"Detroit." I clutch my phone in my hand, watching her fingers fly over the screen of her phone. "Thank you, Farrah."

"Sure…Mick is asking if I want him to send a car here to take you to LAX."

She was able to get a response in less than a minute at six a.m. I forget just how powerful Farrah is sometimes.

"No, I'll take an Uber."

"I'll have Mick text you where to go."

"Okay. Thank you."

Even though I know it's not who she is, I want Farrah to hug me. To tell me it's going to be okay. I'm her center of balance every day, and today, I need that from her.

I turn to leave, knowing she's already said everything she's going to say about it. She's one of the wealthiest, most sought-after actors in the world, but a part of Farrah will always be a little girl who wishes she had parents who loved her.

"I'll keep in touch," I call over my shoulder.

Dalton walks back toward the house with me, neither of us saying a word as JP approaches.

"Morning," he says, grinning. "You guys forget something?"

"I'm going home for a family emergency," I explain.

His smile slides away. "Sorry to hear that. Hope everything goes okay."

"Thanks."

Even JP, who hardly knows me, is showing more concern and compassion than Farrah did.

Dalton goes to my room with me, and as soon as we're inside, he wraps his arms around me and holds me tightly.

"I'll be thinking about you and your dad every minute," he says.

The dam of emotion I've been holding back breaks, and I cry, pressing my face to his chest.

"I haven't seen them since Christmas. And that was just for one day. What if he dies and I'm not there? I've been trying to do the right thing this whole time, and--"

He cuts me off, looking at me intently. "Don't do this to yourself. You've done amazing. One step at a time today, okay? First step is packing anything you might need. I'll call an Uber and then I have to run and grab something from my room. Until you're there, just think about the next thing you have to do to get to him. Do that for me."

I stand up straight and nod. Yes. Breaking it into steps will help me cope with how overwhelmed and helpless I feel right now.

Ten minutes later, Dalton is walking me out to the edge of the security perimeter.

"I have a car here," I murmur. "I should have just taken it."

"You shouldn't be driving right now. An Uber driver can drop you off right at the door."

I look up at him. "Thank you."

"It's gonna be okay." His phone buzzes and he looks at it. "Driver's one minute out."

He carried my overnight bag out for me. He unzips it and slides a box inside.

"This is for you to open later. Don't worry about it for now."

That must be what he needed to get from his room. The sun isn't up yet, so I risk a quick kiss, tears of gratitude and worry gathering in my eyes.

"Thank you, Dalton."

He raises my hand to his lips and kisses the back of it. "Text me when you take off and land, okay? One step at a time."

The car picking me up pulls to a stop next to us. I nod at Dalton. He opens a back-seat door for me and sets my bag in the car once I'm in.

"I'll see you soon," he says.

"Okay."

He stands there, staying as the car pulls away. When I turn to look over my shoulder out the back window, he raises a hand, waving at me. I wave back, already missing his closeness.

I check my phone. No new texts from my mom. I type out a quick message letting her know I'm on my way. Then I look at my bag, my curiosity piqued.

What did he put in my bag? He told me to open it later, but I could use a distraction now.

The distinctive little blue box is from Tiffany. My heart pounds as I open it. There's a folded piece of paper and a beautiful necklace, the pendant a flower shape made of diamonds. I run my finger over it, my lips parting in shock.

It's beautiful. I carefully set the box beside me on the car seat and open the note.

*Alice,*

*I wanted to get you a hundred dozen red roses. But since we're keeping things quiet, I got you this instead. You're so close to me right now, but way too far away.*

*I'm not a man who falls in and out of love easily. I've seen friends fall for women hard and fast, but it never happened for me, until you. I always wanted to keep women at arm's length. But not you. I want to be where you are. If you want to wait, we'll wait. I'm not giving up, though. Be with me, and I'll care for you in every way.*

*Yours,*

*Dalton*

*Yours.* I read the word again and again, smiling despite how worried I am about my dad. Then I read the whole thing again and again after that. He's *mine*. And in my heart, I'm his. Now that I know what this feels like, I can't settle for something average, not in a month, not in a decade.

I don't know what's going to happen, but if I can't have Dalton, I don't want anyone.

*eighteen*

## DALTON

"I'VE MADE SOME GOOD FRIENDS IN MY TIME HERE, and more importantly, I fell in love. And because I have those feelings for her and only her, I can't stay here and pretend to be considering anyone else. It's not right."

Alex bites his fist off camera, his eyes imploring me to say more. When I agreed to go on camera to explain why I was leaving the show, I told him I wouldn't get specific. He's trying everything he can think of to make me change my mind.

"If the two of you are in love, why is she staying and you're going?" he asks.

"I don't speak for her. I only speak for myself. This has been a great experience and I'm grateful for the opportunity. The league trusted me to represent the sport of hockey, and that's an honor. I know my teammates will support my decision. And I guarantee I'll be watching the show to see how things play out."

I indicated with my voice that I was closing out. I wait a couple of seconds and then reach for the microphone clipped inside the collar of my shirt.

"No." Alex rubs his temple, aggravated. "I need more, Dalton. Viewers are going to speculate about every female contestant now, and none of them will be able to focus on anything but which one of them you're leaving the show over. Does she share your feelings? Did she dump you?"

"That's between me and her."

He turns and beats his clipboard on the ground several times, a little spring flying out of it.

"This is a reality show!" He stands back up and whirls to face me. "Don't make me go after you for breach of contract!"

I shrug. "Do what you gotta do, man. I'm not speaking for anyone but me and you're not changing my mind."

I pass the microphone to him, but he won't take

it. After a couple of seconds, I set it on the ground and walk away.

Alice hadn't even been gone for an hour when I started regretting not going with her. I meant it in the letter when I said I wanted to be where she is. Not just in bed. Everywhere.

I should be holding her hand on that plane. Carrying her bag to the car. Standing beside her at the hospital. I didn't think it was possible to fall so hard for someone, but I did. I can't go back to the way I was when I got to the beach house.

I was aloof. Focused entirely on myself. Now there's Alice, and I don't care how anyone but her feels about my leaving the show.

For a few minutes, I thought about asking her if I could come to Detroit. But I need to be there for her, even if I'm sitting in a car in the hospital parking lot because she doesn't want me to meet her family yet.

I go to my room and pack, not worrying about folding my clothes as I stuff them into the two suitcases I brought here. It's a relief to be leaving. I was scheduled to go on a one-on-one date tonight with Hailey and I was dreading it.

Now that Alice is gone, there's no reason for me to be here. I make a final sweep of my bathroom to make sure I got everything and then check my phone. I have a text from my agent.

*Tony: There's a James Morrow at Detroit Memorial. Flight is booked, itinerary in your email. Let me know if you need anything else.*

I text him my thanks. I told him Alice's last name and asked him to see if he could find a patient with her last name at a hospital in Detroit. His assistant is a wizard and I know she's the one who actually did it. She also booked me a flight and arranged for a car to pick me up at the house and take me to the airport and another one to pick me up in Detroit.

Tony's the best. He didn't ask me why I was leaving the show when I texted him about it earlier. He just said he'll read the contract over immediately and handle all communications with the producers and network execs. Now I can focus all my attention on Alice.

"You're leaving?"

I look up and find Farrah glaring at me from the doorway of my bedroom. I cringe inwardly, not in the mood for her bullshit.

"Yeah." I stand up and loop the handle of one bag over my shoulder.

"Why?"

"I don't owe you an explanation, Farrah."

She closes the door and advances on me, her eyes narrowed with fury.

"Go fuck yourself, Dalton. You played me. And I don't understand why. Why not just be honest about who you were really into? I know we have to play along with the drama for the producers, but you could have told me privately that you had no interest in me."

I shrug. "I didn't owe you that. Did you ever tell me who you were and weren't interested in?"

"Is Misty fucking you and Dom separately, or are you guys doing threesomes?"

I gape at her, stunned by the leap she's making. The corners of her lips curl up in a knowing smile.

"There's my answer. You don't want the world to find out you're bi; that's why you're leaving."

I laugh. "You're so far off the mark. I don't give a shit if you make stuff up about me, but Misty doesn't deserve it. Dom doesn't, either, but I'm sure he couldn't give a fuck what a narcissistic actor says about him."

She balks, her eyes widening. "Did you just call me a narcissist?"

My temper flares, but it's not really due to this conversation. It's because of how she treats Alice. It was all I could do to keep quiet this morning when Farrah told Alice she didn't need to go home to be with her family.

"I did, and it's the nicest of the things I'd like to call you. You want to know why you can't figure out who it is I really want, Farrah? It's because you're so fucking wrapped up in yourself. You make everything about you. You don't deserve Alice."

"What does my assistant have to do with any of this?"

I lose my shit. "Alice! Her name is Alice! She's a thousand fucking times more than just your assistant. She's a person, and you take advantage of her. Do you think she wants to work for you every hour of every day, seven days a week? She does it for her family. And then she hardly ever gets to see them because you won't get your own bottles of water out of the fridge for one fucking weekend."

The color drains from her face. "Oh my God. It's *Alice*?"

"Goddamn right it's Alice." I work to keep my voice down so no one can hear us outside this room. "She's beautiful and smart and funny. So fucking generous and selfless. I'd walk through fire for her, and you don't even *see* her. How fucking dare you say *is he dying or something* to her in that bitchy tone earlier? You don't know anything about him. You don't know because *you don't care*."

She leans back, her expression as stricken as if I just slapped her even though we're several feet apart.

"Get out of my way." I glare at her until she turns away and leaves the room, not saying another word.

I close my eyes and blow out a breath as I walk to the stairway. I didn't mean to tell her about me and Alice, but I did, and now I'll have to face the consequences.

If Farrah fires Alice, I'll pay her parents' bills. Hell, I'll pay them anyway. If she'll let me.

THAT EVENING, I'M SITTING IN A WAITING AREA OF Detroit Memorial, a silver-haired woman in the seat across from mine snoring as she sleeps sitting up. I've been here for more than an hour, guilt and nervousness swirling in my gut.

I should've asked Alice if she was okay with this. I came because I wanted to be there for her. But she might not want that. She's going to get a lot of bombshells dropped on her all at once--I left the show and followed her here, and I told Farrah about us.

It's a shit time to drop all that on her when she's so worried about her dad. I'm considering my options, wondering if I should leave when the choice is made for me.

Alice is walking toward a vending machine, and she stops when she sees me, her eyes round with surprise.

I stand up and walk over to her, smiling sheepishly. She's wearing the necklace, which seems like a good sign.

"Surprise," I say, doing weak-ass jazz hands.

She looks around the waiting area, then up and down the hallway. "What's happening? Please tell me there aren't any cameras here."

"No, it's just me. I, uh...left the show." I clear my throat. "But most importantly, how's your dad?"

"He's stable. The doctors think he had a seizure." Her expression softens. "I can't believe you're here."

"I should've asked. I j--"

She cuts me off, throwing herself against me in a hug.

"You're *here*," she says tearfully.

I close my eyes and hold her, relieved. "I meant

it when I said I want to be where you are. I know it's soon and you may not believe this, but...I'm pretty sure I love you."

She stands back and cups my face, tears wetting her cheeks. "I think...I might love you, too."

I just look at her for a couple of seconds, so euphoric I want to pick her up and spin her around the room, announcing to the world that the most incredible woman I've ever known loves me.

Not here, though. Not now, with her dad hospitalized. The most important thing right now is that I support her.

"I'm just gonna sit here and you can come out for hugs whenever," I say.

She smiles and shakes her head. "That might get boring."

"No, I'm good."

Her expression turns serious. "How long is Alex letting you be gone?"

I clear my throat, hoping her feelings don't change when I tell her the truth. "No, I left the show permanently. Alex pitched a fit, but he finally said he'd let me go if I let them film me explaining why."

Alice's hand flies up to cover her mouth. "You did?"

"I said there's only one woman I want, but I didn't say it's you."

Her shoulders relax slightly. "Farrah's going to know. She has to know. Why isn't she blowing up my phone?"

I glance away. "She definitely knows. Because I told her."

Holding my breath, I let the news sink in. Alice looks surprisingly calm about it.

"How did that go?"

I hum a note of unamused laughter. "She thought she had it figured out that I'm bi and I was getting with Misty and Dom."

Alice stutters out a gasp of surprise. "She *what*?"

I shrug. "I mean...if I was into that, I wouldn't be ashamed. Then I called her a narcissist and said some other stuff, and I left."

Alice's jaw drops. "Oh my God, Dalton. Did she explode into ten thousand pieces? Is she splattered all over the beach house walls right now?"

"She's fine. Probably pissed off, but fine." I put my hands on her shoulders, holding her gaze. "I'm sorry. It wasn't my place to tell her."

Alice puts a hand on my forearm and squeezes

it gently. "It's okay. She would've found out anyway."

"I've got you on money, okay? I don't want you worrying about your dad's care. I've got more than enough to take care of everything."

She nods slowly. "I've been thinking about it. Will's getting paid now, and I have some money in the bank. I invested a little that I can cash out if I need it, and I can get another job. It'll be okay. I knew when I made the decision to come here that I might not be working for Farrah anymore."

"Don't go back to her. You deserve to have a life."

She runs a fingertip over the pendant of her necklace, a smile playing on her lips. "Now that I know what it's like to have a life, I think I like it."

I run my thumb over her jawline. "Good. Because we're just getting started, babe."

She takes my hand, arching her brows. "Are you ready to meet my parents?"

"Are you sure?"

She nods. "It's been a whirlwind, but if you're in, I'm in."

I give her hand a light squeeze. "I'm all in. With everything I've got."

*nineteen*

ALICE

Three Weeks Later

"That. Better. Be. A. Margarita."

I hold up my dad's bag of liquid nutrition, laughing lightly. "How'd you know? I'm even salting the rim of your G-tube. But not until later, when Mom is here to help me with it."

He's been home for almost ten days now, his condition more fragile than before. The doctors had to put a gastrostomy tube in his stomach so he can be fed a liquid diet that gives him the nutrients he needs and helps protect his deteriorating kidneys.

Once his bag is stored in the small refrigerator in his room, I tuck his covers around him, his eyes already closing. I kiss his forehead, double-checking that the large call button on the side of the hospital bed in his bedroom is within his reach.

"Call if you need anything, Dad. You better sleep while you can. Dalton has another game picked out to watch tonight."

His lips twitch, which is him smiling. For the past few evenings, Dalton has carried my dad out to the living room and streamed one of his old hockey games on our TV. He's teaching us about hockey and all the little things he sees himself doing on film that he's always working on.

My dad loves every minute of it. My mom says he works harder at therapy when Dalton takes him. It's just been the two of them for a long time, and my parents are thrilled to have time to get to know Dalton and catch up with me.

I close his bedroom door and find Dalton in the kitchen making sandwiches for our lunch.

"You're not tired of my mom's chicken salad?"

He grins at me. "Are you kidding? I love this stuff. She should package it and sell it."

I walk over to him and hug him from behind. He raves about my mom's cooking, and she eats up every word. I think he genuinely does love it, because he has a bowl of chicken salad on the counter with a fork in it that he's snacking on while he makes the sandwiches.

"Did you notice that since I don't like the grapes in the chicken salad, and you love the grapes in it, she put more grapes in it this time?" I roll my eyes as I walk over to the dishwasher.

"I'm a growing boy, babe. Maria knows it."

My mom adores Dalton. In the three weeks he's been staying with us at their house, he's done all the grocery shopping, taken over mowing and trimming the yard, and fixed the leaky roof on their shed. Not to mention his help with Dad's care.

Dalton and I have been taking Dad to his therapy and doctor appointments in what Dalton calls my parents' "party van." Once we've used the wheelchair lift to get him inside and secure him, Dalton gets behind the wheel of the van and asks Dad where he wants to go. He lists off ideas like casinos, gentlemen's clubs, and the golf course.

Dad has always had a great sense of humor, and his lips twitch with mirth as Dalton pretends he's taking Dad to play poker or shoot nine holes.

"Speaking of my mom, where is she?" I ask as I unload clean dishes from the dishwasher.

"She went to get a pedicure."

"Oh, that's right. She's getting her hair done, too. She's so excited about Will coming for the weekend."

Dalton sets my plate down in front of me on the counter, my chicken salad sandwich on white cut into two neat triangles. "I finally get to find out if you're the good twin or the evil twin."

"Let me know what you decide," I quip. "You're free to share a bed with Will if you want."

He wraps his arms around my waist from behind as I put a bowl in a kitchen cabinet.

"You'd miss me too much, Miss Morrow." He holds me close, my back to his chest, and I let my head fall back on his shoulder.

"You do have certain talents I've grown fond of," I say playfully.

It took me more than a week to convince him to have sex with me in my parents' house. He said he felt like a high school kid who was worried about getting busted.

We've become great at stealthy sex. Dalton is particularly skilled with his hands, using one to slowly tease me while he covers my mouth with his other one to conceal my moans.

He kisses my neck, gently tugging on my earlobe with his teeth. I get that familiar swirl of desire in my stomach for him, his hand sliding underneath the hem of my T-shirt.

"You know, we could--"

The ringing of the doorbell cuts me off. I turn and look at him, grabbing a handful of the front of his T-shirt and pulling lightly.

"Probably just a delivery. Want to meet me in the bedroom?"

His gaze darkens. "You know I do."

I close the dishwasher door, leaving the rest of the clean dishes for later. Dalton is scarfing his sandwich as I go into the living room and open the front door.

Farrah is standing there, a vase full of colorful flowers in her hands.

"Hey," she says, her eyes locking with mine.

"Hi."

My heart races as it sets in that she's really here, at my parents' home. It's nothing like the mansions she owns.

"How's your dad doing?" she asks.

I'm too stunned to answer for a second. Farrah

has never asked how *I* was doing, let alone one of my family members.

"He's home. Still himself inside and able to communicate with us."

She nods. "Good. I brought these for him."

She's dressed in black leggings and a plain, lightweight white T-shirt, her long blond hair flowing out of the back of a baseball cap. This is how she dresses for plane flights, and she also has on the big sunglasses that help disguise her a bit. It looks like she's not wearing makeup, which is rare for her.

"Do you want to come inside?"

She hesitates. "I don't want to intrude. But could we maybe...talk out here for a little bit?"

I step aside. "You're not intruding. Come in."

Nodding, she steps in, taking in my parents' small, cozy living room that's swallowed up by a couch and two recliners. Photos of me and Will growing up line the walls. An afghan made decades ago by my grandma is folded neatly and hung over the back of the worn couch they've had since I was a kid.

Dalton comes in from the kitchen, his gaze shooting between me and Farrah.

"Hey, Farrah," he says in a neutral tone.

"Hey. Can I give these to you?"

"Yeah." He comes over and takes the vase of flowers. "You want a chicken salad sandwich? Or a drink?"

I love that he's so comfortable here. And that even though he's pissed at Farrah, he seems to know how much pride she had to swallow to show up here.

"I'm good, thanks."

He nods, looking at me. "I'll be upstairs."

Farrah sits down on one end of the couch, and I sit down on the other end. It's weird. Having the two parts of my life that have always been so separate colliding out of nowhere.

"I owe you an apology, Alice."

"You don't have to apologize. I know Dalton said some things, but I knew what working for you meant, and you've been very generous with money. It's changed my family's lives."

She shakes her head, tears welling in her eyes as she smiles sadly. "It's so like you to let me off the hook. But Dalton was right. I spent the rest of my time on the show thinking about our relationship."

"So you're done with filming?"

She nods. "Spoiler alert--I didn't end up with

anyone. You can't tell anyone that, of course, because of the NDAs we signed."

"I won't."

She breaks out into the dazzling smile that has graced many movie posters. "I think Misty and Dom are going to end up married. Who saw that coming?"

I get a warm feeling as I remember the sweet gymnast who deserves all the happiness in the world from what I can see. "Good for Misty."

She sighs heavily. "Guess it's obvious I'm new to apologizing."

I close the distance between us, a lump in my throat as I cover her hand with one of mine.

"I thought you'd hate me for leaving. If you don't, we're good."

Her gaze falls to her lap, where a tear drops onto the back of my hand. "I could never hate you, Alice. You're my best friend. I..." Her voice wavers and she clears her throat. "I love you."

"I love you, too." My own eyes flood with tears. "And you're my best friend."

She looks up at me, a wet trail running down each of her cheeks. "Really? Even though our relationship has been completely about me?"

"It hasn't. You watched *Mean Girls* for me. You

took me to that French bakery so I could try things even though you didn't want any of it."

She laughs softly. "I wanted *all of it*."

"You've always included me in your adventures. I'm not some sad little assistant who waits in the trailer while you're skydiving and going on safaris. We've done things together that I never would have dreamed of doing without you."

She covers my hand with her other one. "Thank you for being so gracious. But I have to say this just so I know I did this the right way. I've treated you unfairly and you're the last person in my life who--," She pauses to take a breath after her voice breaks. "Who deserved that. I'm sorry. And I'm so happy Dalton realized the most amazing woman on that show--the greatest catch--was you."

We're both crying as I wrap my arms around her in a hug.

"Of course I forgive you. I'm so happy you're not...mad at me."

She pulls away, wiping her cheeks. "I need to work on myself. I'm not signing the contract for the next movie."

"You're not?"

She shakes her head, looking amused. "I'm going to rehab."

My eyes widen with surprise. "Rehab? You don't drink alcohol or use drugs."

"You can pay fancy rehab places to treat you for literally anything, and they'll take your twenty thousand a week. Can you believe that? So I'm going to narcissism rehab."

My jaw drops. Farrah has become shockingly self-aware in the three weeks we've been apart.

"Farrah, that's..." I stumble, unable to come up with a word for it.

She laughs. "It's fucked. But I'm really looking forward to it. They're going to teach me how to have 'healthy, reciprocal relationships.'" She air quotes the words. "I'm hoping to practice on that with you."

A wave of trepidation hits me. "I meant it about loving you, but the doctors have said my dad's going to decline faster than before, and I need to be here with my parents right now."

"I know. I get it. You should be here. Jackie is depositing two years' worth of your salary into your account on your next payday."

My stomach drops. "No, you don't--"

She cuts me off mid-sentence. "Stop. It's done, and if you or your family need anything else, *anything at all*, you call Jackie and she'll take care of getting you more."

I'm too overcome with emotion to respond to her for a few seconds. When I do manage, it's through tears. "Thank you. That means the world to me."

"I'll be in rehab for sixteen weeks. I start on Monday."

I picture Farrah in a plain room with no luxuries. No one bringing her lavender water. No one running to a local gas station to buy a Kit Kat just so she can sniff it.

"Well...at least the main topic of conversation will be *you*," I quip.

She laughs heartily at that. "That's a fair point. Would it be okay if I call you when I'm allowed to?"

"Of course. Please call me. I've been sad about not having you in my life anymore. I never wanted that."

She puts an arm around me. "You're not getting rid of me that easily. Even though you aren't my assistant anymore, I'm hoping that at some point, you'll consider becoming my business manager. You know the business, you know me, and I trust you completely."

"Really?"

"Yes. You can do it entirely remotely if you want. Or you can travel with me every now and then, but only if you want to. I'll never ask you to do anything but business manager work. And if you don't want to do that, I respect it and still want to keep you as my best friend."

I don't even have to think about it. "I'm interested. But not while my dad is..."

I look away, unable to finish the sentence.

"The job is yours. In six months or in six years."

I nod, warming to the idea as it sets in. She's flawed, but I do love Farrah. Getting to have my own life and still be close with her is something I never dreamed possible.

"So what are you doing until you start narcissist rehab?"

A little snort comes out when she laughs. "You're going to call it that until we're old and gray, aren't you?"

"Definitely."

"I'm staying at a hotel in downtown Detroit. I fly out early Monday for Bali."

"Bali?" I give her a wistful look. "I want to go, too."

"I know. I'll scope out a spa for us to stay at when I finish. If you can."

"Well, I'd love for you to meet my family. My mom made lasagna for dinner, which I know you don't eat, but you're welcome to come over and...have some water?"

Her smile reaches her eyes, warm and sincere. "I would love to eat your mom's lasagna. You don't think Dalton would mind?"

I wave a hand. "Of course not."

"I'm happy for you. Really, really happy. He better treat you right."

My fingertips reflexively move over the flower pendant. I still read the letter he wrote me at least once a day. "He does. I'll have more time on my hands when his hockey season starts, but for now, I'm just enjoying having him all to myself." I look over at the stairway. "Speaking of Dalton, I'm going to go get him. I'm making an apple pie for tonight, so we can all catch up while I work on it."

"Great."

I'm almost all the way up the stairs when the doorbell rings. I jog down a couple of stairs and stop, leaning down to look out the window for a delivery truck.

"You want me to...?" Farrah is standing a few

feet in front of the door, looking at me.

"Yeah, thanks."

She opens the door with a smile. I can't see who's on the other side as she says, "Can I help you?"

"I hope so. This is my parents' house."

Her jaw drops. "Oh, sorry! Come in. Hi, I'm Farrah."

My twin walks into the house, a bag slung over his shoulder. At six-three with broad shoulders and a lean waistline, he makes his blue scrubs look good. His dark hair is cut short and he has a couple days' worth of stubble.

Dalton joins me on the stairway, sliding an arm around my waist.

"Hi Farrah, I'm Will Morrow."

Farrah shakes his hand, her expression lighting up as they shake hands, seconds ticking by as they stare at each other. Will looks equally mesmerized by her.

"It's really nice to meet you," she finally says.

"You, too. If I'd known you were going to be here, I would've cleaned up. I came straight from work."

She smiles up at him, her hand still in his. "No. I think you look...perfect."

Book 2 - Pike

Book 3 - Pax

**St. Lous Mavericks series**

Book 1 - Hard Fall

Book 2 - Hard Limit

Book 3 - Hard Pass

Book 4 - Hard Luck

Book 5 - Hard Hit

**Fire on Ice Series**

Book 1 - Bound

Book 2 - Captive

Book 3 - Edge

Book 4 - Drive

Book 5 - Release

**On the Line Series**

Book 1 - Killian

Book 2 - Bennett

**Lockhart Brothers Series**

Book 1 - Deep Down

Book 2 - In Deep

Book 3 - Drawn Deeper

Book 4 - Hidden Depth

**FILTHY SERIES**

Book 1 - Dirty Work

Book 2 - Dirty Secret

Book 3 - Dirty Defiance

**STANDALONES**

Come Closer

Buried

Sweet Sixteen

His

Alpha Mail

Healing Touch

Barely Breathing

Exiled

Unspoken

Brenda Rothert lives in Central Illinois with her husband, children and three dogs. She loves to hear from readers through her website or her Facebook Group, Rothert's Readers.

Keep up with all the latest on Brenda's books and get bonus content by signing up for her newsletter HERE.